They

A part of Lucas w...
finished.

He looked into her eyes and saw the passion-glazed stare of a woman completely undone and should have felt a jolt of satisfaction for a plan that was coming together all too well.

Instead, all he felt was more want. More need.

Her blue eyes were shining with every ounce of passion that was flaring inside him. The smoldering fire between them leaped to life like an inferno.

Heartbeat pounding, he took her mouth again. And then Lucas did the only thing he could. He moved inside her again and heard her groan of satisfaction as his reward.

This wasn't seduction anymore.

This was *need*. Crashing, burning desperation—and it wouldn't be denied.

* * *

To find out more about Harlequin Desire's upcoming books and to chat with authors and editors, become a fan of Harlequin Desire on Facebook, www.facebook.com/HarlequinDesire, or follow us on Twitter, www.twitter.com/desireeditors!

Dear Reader,

Writing a continuing family series, like the Kings of California, is as much fun for the writer as it is for the reader. We all love revisiting earlier characters. It's like having a nice long chat with an old friend you haven't seen for a while. I especially enjoy doing groups of two or three at a time that are more connected than just by their family name.

In *Ready for King's Seduction,* Lucas King gets his heroine. Not too long ago, he stood on the sidelines, snickering at his brother Rafe as he fell in love with Katie Charles, the Cookie Queen. Now, it's Rafe's turn to chuckle.

Lucas meets Rose Clancy, the younger sister of his ex-friend, and concocts a plan. He's determined to get back at Rose's brother for betraying the King brothers.

Rose Clancy, though, isn't the wide-eyed innocent that Lucas remembers. She's had a hard time of it, but she's survived and rebuilt her life. Now she teaches people how to cook in their own homes. When Lucas hires her, Rose agrees because she can use all the clients she can get.

But while Rose teaches cooking, Lucas is teaching her passion, and neither of them is prepared for what they find.

I really hope you enjoy *Ready for King's Seduction!* Next up is Sean King's book, *The Temporary Mrs. King,* and I hope you'll watch for it! Follow me on Facebook and Twitter and let me know what you think!

Happy reading,

Maureen

MAUREEN CHILD

READY FOR KING'S SEDUCTION

ISBN-13: 978-0-373-73126-8

READY FOR KING'S SEDUCTION

MAUREEN CHILD

is a California native who loves to travel. Every chance they get, she and her husband are taking off on another research trip. The author of more than sixty books, Maureen loves a happy ending and still swears that she has the best job in the world. She lives in Southern California with her husband, two children and a golden retriever with delusions of grandeur. Visit Maureen's website, www.maureenchild.com.

To my mother-in-law, Mary Ann Child,
for years of laughter and love and adventures.
I couldn't love you more.

One

"There's something you don't see every day."

"What are you talking about?" Lucas King stepped through his front door onto the wide porch and handed his younger brother a beer. Just for a second, he took the time to admire the view of the Pacific Ocean, across the street. The sun was setting, staining the dark blue water deep shades of crimson and gold. He settled into the closest chair and took a sip of his beer.

Sean grinned and pointed. "That. Look what just pulled up outside your neighbor's house."

Lucas shifted his gaze to Ocean Boulevard and his eyes widened. A dark blue minivan was parked in front of the house next door. Ordinarily, no big deal—except for the giant covered skillet on the roof.

"What the—"

"Check out the sign on the side," Sean said, laughing.

"'Home cooking taught at home,'" Lucas recited,

shaking his head. "So the sign on the side of the car in bright yellow paint wasn't enough? They had to stick a pan on top?"

Sean was still laughing as he took a sip of his beer. "Not exactly aerodynamic."

"It looks ridiculous," Lucas said, wondering what kind of person would have so little pride they'd be willing to drive the thing. "Who the hell runs a business like that, anyway?"

"Mmm..." Sean's tone changed as the minivan's door opened and the driver stepped out into the street. "Whoever she is, she can teach me whatever she wants to."

Lucas rolled his eyes even as he shifted his gaze back to the ocean. Big surprise. Sean was always willing and eager for the next woman to roll into his life. Give him five minutes with Pan-on-the-Car Woman, Lucas told himself, and Sean would have a weekend getaway scheduled. Well, Sean was welcome to the stream of women entering and exiting his life. Lucas liked his life a little more orderly.

Only half listening to Sean's running commentary, Lucas ignored the woman and the car and focused on the stretch of water sliding toward the horizon. This is what he loved about where he lived. Every night after work, he could come out to the porch, have a beer, stare out at the water and let the world slip away for a while. Usually though, he thought—Sean's voice an annoying buzz of sound in the background—he was alone.

Here, he didn't have to be on top of King Construction. Here, no one was hounding him for a meeting or to fix something gone wrong with permits. There were no needy customers to placate and no hurry to accomplish a damn thing.

Oh, he liked his work. He and his brothers Rafe and Sean had built King Construction into the biggest firm of its kind on the west coast. But damned if it didn't feel good to come home and let it all go for a while.

"Always did like a blonde," Sean was saying. "And a tall one, too."

Lucas snorted. "Blondes, redheads, brunettes. Your problem is you like 'em all."

"Yeah? Your problem is you're too damn picky. When was the last time you called a woman who wasn't a customer?" Sean kicked back in his chair, setting his feet on the stone porch-balcony rail in front of them.

"None of your business," Lucas muttered.

"Hell. That long? No wonder you're such a pain in the ass lately." Sean took another drink of his beer. "What you need is a little female attention and if you've got eyes in your head, one look at this blonde and you'll be ready to go."

Lucas sighed and surrendered to the inevitable. Sean wasn't going to shut up about the woman, so Lucas might as well get a good look at her for himself. "No way," he muttered.

"Huh?" Sean glanced at him.

"I don't believe this," Lucas said, more to himself than to his brother. He stood up, eyes locked on the tall, curvy blonde hurrying around the front of her car. Her long hair was pulled into a ponytail at the base of her neck, the wind whipping her hair into a frenzy. Her skin was pale and, he knew, dusted with freckles across her nose and cheeks. He couldn't see her eyes from here, but he knew they were a deep summer blue. Her mouth was wide and curved easily into a smile, and her laugh was infectious as hell.

He hadn't seen her in two years and seeing her *now* sent a near electric current sizzling through him. Lucas watched her open the sliding side door, then bend over to reach inside.

Instantly, he shifted his gaze to the curve of her behind, defined by the tight black jeans she wore. That buzz of something inside him heightened into a crackling, pulsing energy.

"What's going on?" Sean pushed out of his chair to stand beside his brother. "You know her?"

"I used to," Lucas admitted. Not as well as he had wanted to at the time, of course. A guy just didn't make moves on his friend's sister.

"Great. How about you introduce me to tall, blonde and luscious—"

Lucas glared at him.

Sean nodded and held up both hands. "Okay then, never mind. So who is she?"

"Rose Clancy."

Sean's eyebrows went up high enough that the shock of black hair falling across his forehead completely hid them. Then he turned and looked at the blonde, still fishing around inside her van. "*That's* Dave Clancy's little sister?"

"That's her."

"The one he always claimed was practically a saint? Good? Sweet? Pure as the driven snow?"

"The very one," Lucas muttered, his gaze now narrowed on her as he remembered all the times he had listened to his ex-friend Dave brag about his baby sister.

The Clancy family ran a rival construction company.

Well, rivals in the sense that they were all in the same business. In Lucas's mind, there had never really been a contest between them. King Construction was the best firm in the state, but Clancy came in a close second.

He and Dave had met at a chamber-of-commerce meeting and had immediately hit it off. They'd been friends as well as friendly competitors. Until the day two years ago when Lucas finally figured out that Dave Clancy was a liar and a thief.

"Didn't I hear that Rose got a divorce last year from that ass she married?"

"Yeah," Lucas said, still watching as Rose hurried back to her van for more supplies. "I heard she divorced him. Weren't married long, either."

Long enough, though, Lucas thought, to discover her husband was a cheating dog that should have been neutered for the good of humanity. Funny that her so protective older brother hadn't bothered to save her from a bad marriage.

Rose gathered up a few more things, then slid the door closed, beeped the lock and headed for the house again. She never once glanced at her surroundings, so she didn't notice Lucas and Sean standing on the porch staring at her.

"What're you planning?" Sean asked and Lucas turned his head to look at him.

"Not planning a thing," he lied as his mind raced with sudden possibilities.

"Right. Sell that to somebody who doesn't know you."

"Don't you have a date tonight?" Lucas asked.

"Yeah, I do."

"Then maybe you should go."

"Translation," Sean said wryly, "you don't want to tell me what you're thinking about doing."

Lucas grinned. "Smart man."

Shaking his head, Sean set his half-empty bottle of beer down onto the stone rail and headed for the steps. He paused, though, to look over his shoulder at his brother. "You know, it was *Dave* who cheated us. Not his sister."

Lucas met Sean's gaze evenly, his eyes giving away nothing he was feeling. "Did I say anything about Dave?"

"No," Sean admitted. "But I know how your mind works."

"Is that a fact?"

"It is." Sean tipped his head to one side and studied him for a long minute. "Kings don't like getting screwed. But Lucas King takes betrayal as a personal insult."

"Isn't it?" Lucas looked away from his brother, back to his neighbor's empty front yard and Rose's ridiculous van.

Dave Clancy had been a friend. Someone Lucas trusted. And he didn't trust many people. Having that friend turn on him had cut deep and damned if he'd apologize for still being angry.

"Dave cheated all of us," Lucas reminded his brother. "He paid one of our employees to give him insider information and then he went out and undercut our bids on four different projects. I call that pretty damn personal."

"We never found any proof of that."

"Yeah? I got my proof when Lane Thomas left us to go to work for Dave's outfit and suddenly the undercutting stopped. Coincidence?"

"Fine." Sean pushed one hand through his hair and

shrugged. "All I'm saying is taking your anger out on Rose won't do a damn thing to settle up with Dave."

"Who says I'm taking anything out on anybody?" Lucas asked.

"So you're not planning on a little payback?"

"I'll see you at work tomorrow, Sean."

"No way does this end well," Sean told him, then turned and headed down the front walk to his car.

Lucas dismissed his brother in the next minute. "It won't end well for the Clancys," he murmured thoughtfully. "That's for damn sure."

Rose waved goodbye to the woman standing in the doorway and didn't let her smile fade until the front door was closed. The sidewalk was brightly lit and the streetlights on Ocean Boulevard gave off a soft yellow glow, so she didn't mind the darkness. It was actually a relief to get out into the cold, crisp night and away from the lingering smell of burned onions.

Kathy Robertson was determined to become a good cook—which made her an excellent client—but it wasn't going to be easy. Still, that meant Mrs. Robertson was going to be a long-term project, and that meant solvency for Rose's burgeoning business. A good thing. Smiling to herself, Rose stacked her supplies back in her van, slid the door closed and then jumped when a man's voice spoke up from behind her.

"Been a while."

She spun around, hand to her chest, and looked up at a man she hadn't seen in two years. Not since he and her older brother had cut off all communication. As soon as her heart slid out of her throat, it started pounding in excitement. "Lucas?"

He was leaning against her van. How had he walked

up without her being aware of it? Now that she knew he was there, her skin was prickling and her nerve endings were standing up straight, dancing in appreciation. He was wearing a pullover red sweater over a white T-shirt and black jeans. His boots were scuffed and his black hair was ruffled by the wind. His jaw boasted the shadow of a beard and his blue eyes were fixed on her.

"You scared me to death," she admitted when she could find her voice again.

"Sorry," he said, but didn't sound apologetic at all. "Didn't mean to startle you. But I wanted to talk to you before you left."

"Where'd you come from?" She glanced up and down the street, idly noting the steady stream of traffic.

"I live next door," he told her, jerking his thumb toward the two-story house boasting a wide, stone front porch.

"I didn't know," she said, which was a good thing. Because she might not have taken the Robertsons on as customers if she had known Lucas King lived right beside them.

A few years ago, she had spent a lot of time day-dreaming about this man. It hadn't gone any further than that, of course, because her brother, Dave, had made sure to keep Lucas at a distance from her. Still, it hadn't been easy to put Lucas out of her mind. He continued to sneak back in at unexpected moments. Seeing him again was only going to refuel those old daydreams and make *not* thinking about him even more difficult.

But he'd made himself very clear three years ago. He hadn't been interested in her enough then to go against her brother's interference and there was no reason to think that had changed. Besides, she'd been through a lot in the past few years. She wasn't the easily charmed or foolishly romantic girl she had been.

Sure, her mind taunted slyly, *that's why your heart's still pounding and your palms are damp. Because you're so cool and controlled.*

Frowning at her own inner turmoil, she missed what Lucas said and was forced to ask, "What?"

He pushed away from the car, stuffed his hands into his back pockets and repeated, "I said, I'm glad to see you're teaching Kathy to cook. I've been to dinner at their place. Not pretty."

Wryly, Rose was forced to admit, "She is...challenging. But she's determined to improve, and that's good for all of us."

Nodding his head, he glanced at the skillet on top of her car. "Interesting advertisement."

She knew what he must be thinking, but Rose liked her skillet. An artist friend had made it for her and attached it to the roof of the van. "I think it's quirky."

"That's one word for it," he said.

Instantly, her back went up. She'd had to defend her new business to her older brother, and she wasn't going to do the same with Dave's ex-friend. Which reminded her of the fact that Dave and Lucas weren't even speaking anymore. So why was Lucas talking to her now?

She pushed windblown hair off her face and asked, "Was there something you wanted, Lucas?"

He looked at her for a long, silent moment, those blue eyes of his shadowed in the dim light. But his stare was just as powerful as it had once been, and Rose felt her heartbeat quicken again in response. It was an involuntary reaction, she told herself firmly, and refused to acknowledge it further.

"Actually," he said, "there is. You teach cooking classes in people's homes, right?"

"Yeah..."

"Then I want to hire you."

She hadn't expected that and wasn't entirely sure what to make of it. Lucas King was one of the wealthiest men in America. He could employ a dozen chefs and never once have to enter his own kitchen if he didn't want to. So why learn to cook for himself?

"Why?"

He pulled his hands free of his pockets and folded his arms across his broad chest. "I should think that would be self-evident. I want to know how to cook."

"Yeah, I get that," she said, still not willing to believe that he was serious. "What I don't understand is why you want to hire me."

"Because I don't want to have to go out to take classes. You coming to my home is more convenient."

"Uh-huh." She was thinking fast and trying to see the trap in what he was saying, but she just couldn't. Maybe he was being sincere. Maybe he really did want to learn how to cook for himself and seeing her here tonight had just been a happy accident.

But even as she thought it, Rose told herself there had to be more to it than that. As far as she knew, Lucas and her brother hadn't spoken in a couple of years. Though she had tried to find out from Dave what had gone wrong in their friendship, her brother hadn't told her a thing.

All he'd been willing to say was that Lucas King was out of their lives and she had better leave it that way.

If Lucas felt the same, and she had no reason to think he didn't, why was he trying to hire her?

"How much do you charge?" Lucas asked, splintering her thoughts.

She told him and he nodded. "I'll pay you twice your usual rate."

"What? Why would you do that?"

"For your undivided attention," he told her. "I'd want you here every night. Teaching me."

She took a quick breath and tried to put out the flickering flames in the pit of her stomach. Every night. Teaching him. It sounded way more sexual than it should have.

"I have other clients," she told him, though the truth was, her new business was barely up and sputtering. Besides Kathy Robertson, there were only three other women who had hired her so far and they were only once-a-month commitments.

"Three times your usual rate," he countered, his gaze fixed on her, his expression unreadable.

Rose blew out a breath she hadn't realized she'd been holding. With that kind of money, she could get a running start on building her business. Yes, she didn't *have* to struggle. She was a Clancy after all, and if she was in deep trouble, she would only have to tell Dave she needed money.

But she really didn't want to go to her brother. And she'd already invested everything she had into her business. So it was sink or swim. Lucas's offer would make it much easier to stay afloat.

"You're not making it easy to say no," she admitted.

"Glad to hear it," Lucas said.

She took a deep breath and, shaking her head slowly, heard herself say, "I don't know, Lucas. If Dave found out about this—"

"So," he interrupted, "you're still letting your older brother run your life, is that it?"

Her head snapped up, her gaze locked with his and a fast spurt of anger shot through her. "Dave has never run my life."

"Not how he saw it."

"Things change."

"Do they?" Lucas prodded. "Then take my offer."

Frowning to herself, Rose knew she was being manipulated and she didn't like it. But she also didn't like the fact that Lucas had a point. If she turned his offer down, she was kowtowing to the older brother who already thought he had a right to run her life.

Well, times had changed and so had Rose. She was a grown-up. She had survived the loss of her father, the disintegration of a bad marriage and the bossiness of a brother who thought he knew best. She could handle Lucas King and the still-sizzling attraction she felt for him.

"All right," she said, holding out her right hand, "it's a deal."

His hand enveloped hers in a warm shake that sent tendrils of something deliciously wicked streaming through her system. He gave her a half smile and said, "Great. We'll start tomorrow. Six work for you?"

He let her go but her skin was still buzzing from his touch when she mumbled, "Yeah. Six is fine."

"See you then." Lucas turned and headed back to his house and Rose watched him go.

Leaning against her car, she ordered her heartbeat to slow down and told her stomach to stop spinning.

Neither of those commands had the slightest effect on her.

When he disappeared into his house, Rose shook her head slowly and whispered, "I'm in *so* much trouble."

Two

"Real men don't eat mushrooms," Lucas pointed out the next night as he sliced into the tiny white buttons. "They're not even vegetables. Aren't they a fungus?"

Rose laughed, and Lucas stilled for a second, listening to the sound of it. Just as he remembered, that laugh of hers was damned infectious. Made a man want to smile in response, then pull her in close for a long, deep, wet kiss that would end in—

"Technically, yes," she said, when she'd stopped laughing at him long enough to speak. "They are fungi. For a long time, they were considered vegetables, but then researchers discovered they weren't plant or animal, but their own species."

"Great. And I'm going to eat them, why?"

Lucas waited for it and wasn't disappointed. She laughed again and something inside him shifted, expanded.

Their first cooking lesson was going more smoothly than he'd expected. Sure, there had been some tension when she first arrived, but that had dissipated quickly enough when she got a look at his kitchen. He smiled to himself when he realized that she was the first woman to be seduced by his subzero fridge and Viking stove.

Hell, when he remodeled the house after buying it five years ago, he had insisted on top-of-the-line, and the designer had been given free rein in the kitchen. From the bamboo flooring to the glass-fronted cabinets, the granite counters and workstations and the island sink, the kitchen was the kind of room every cook dreamed of.

And the most Lucas had ever made in it himself was the occasional plate of bacon and eggs.

Now, though, he thought as he watched Rose moving through the room, he would always see her here. He would hear the echoes of her laughter. See the way she practically danced around the room with a sort of balletic grace. She cooed over the copper pots and pans and sighed deeply when she first opened the nearly empty butler's pantry.

She might have been a little nervous when she'd first arrived, but in his kitchen, she was right at home.

"We're using button mushrooms because they're the most common. You can find them in any grocery store and they add just enough flavor to any dish to give it a hint of something…more."

"More fungus. Great." He shook his head, reminded himself that he wasn't here to enjoy himself—or her. He had set this up as a way of paying back a friend for the kind of betrayal that Lucas never forgave. Rose wasn't a date.

She was a tool.

Grimly, he went back to the task of slicing mushrooms while Rose gathered up the supplies she'd brought along and set them out on the cooking island.

"I brought enough with me for tonight's lesson," she said, "because this was all so sudden I figured you wouldn't have the right ingredients."

"Good call," he said, his knife sliding through button after button.

"But it's just a crime that you have this amazing kitchen and nothing in it," she said with a long sigh. Shaking her head, she looked around the room as if studying an abandoned puppy and wondering how to find it a good home. "I'm going to leave a list of supplies for you to pick up. With a well-stocked pantry and refrigerator, you'll always have options."

He lifted his head to look at her, and their eyes locked. A second or two of pulsing tension passed before he said, "Until I learn how to cook, being well-stocked really isn't necessary, is it?"

She plopped one hand on her hip. "How am I supposed to teach you how to cook if there's nothing in your house to cook *with?*"

"Good point again," he muttered, then rallied. "Okay, leave your list. I'll have my secretary take care of getting whatever you think I need."

"Your secretary."

He frowned at her. "Something wrong with that?"

"Oh, no," she said, lifting both hands in surrender. "Just typical, that's all."

"Typical of what?"

"Men like you. And Dave."

"Excuse me?" He stiffened. "I'm nothing like your brother, let's get that straight right now."

Now it was her turn to stiffen up, and Lucas noted

the flash of emotion in her eyes. "Look, I know you and Dave don't speak anymore—"

"That's right, we don't," he said, cutting her off before she could try to do something as fruitless as attempt to salvage a friendship that was dead to him.

It was good that she'd brought him up, though. Good to reinforce the fact that Rose was the sister of his enemy. A man he had once trusted. And the only reason Rose was standing here, driving him insane with her soft scent of lemons, was that Lucas was going to use her to get back at the man who had betrayed him. Revenge. Pure. Simple.

Sweet.

A minute or two of strained silence passed before she said, "All I meant was that men like *you* most often delegate work to your secretaries—even when it's not something that's really part of their job descriptions."

He looked at her, the knife in his hand still. "My secretary's job description includes pretty much whatever I say it does."

"Uh-huh. Even grocery shopping?"

"There's something wrong with that?"

She leaned both hands on the cooking island's cool granite surface. Her skin looked even paler against the gleaming black stone. "How will you know what to get in the future? You plan to always have your secretary do the work for you?"

Actually, it sounded like a good plan to Lucas. If he wanted to grocery shop, there would be actual food in his house right now. But why would he when there was a great diner just a half block away and enough restaurants in the city of Long Beach that a man wouldn't have to eat at the same place twice during a six-month span?

Rose shook her head. "Maybe I should be giving your secretary the lessons."

Okay, that was a little insulting. "Fine," he said. "I'll get the groceries. Make a list, and I'll take care of it before tomorrow night."

Smiling, she said, "How about we do it together tomorrow? We'll call it part of the lesson. I'll show you how to choose your produce and what to look for at the meat counter."

Lucas nodded, and she smiled even wider. Grocery shopping. Not exactly a high-end kind of date, he told himself, but then he wasn't dating her, either. This was a planned seduction. What he wanted to do was get her off guard and keep her there. Then, when she was relaxed enough, he'd tumble her into bed. Once that was done, Lucas would tell her brother just how good she had been, and he'd have the kind of revenge that would tear at Dave Clancy for the rest of his life.

"But for now," Rose was saying, "you finish slicing the mushrooms, then I want you to chop three table-spoons of fresh parsley."

He paused and frowned. "Isn't parsley the decoration on plates that no one ever eats?"

"Some of us actually do eat it."

"Amazing," he muttered, but went back to his task. While he worked, he managed to keep one eye on Rose as she explored his kitchen. She drew down plates and wineglasses from the cupboards, opened up the fridge and grabbed the sour cream, cheese and butter she'd brought with her for tonight's recipe.

In a few minutes, they were working together amiably. But when she turned on the radio and soft jazz spilled from the speakers, Lucas began to worry.

He was actually enjoying himself.

And that wasn't part of the plan.

"So?" Rose asked an hour later, "what do you think?"

She was sitting opposite him at the glass-topped table at the far end of the kitchen. Beside them was a bay window that overlooked a wide backyard. The garden lights were on, spilling small circles of golden radiance across the grass and neatly tended flowerbeds. The winter garden was sparse, but even in the dimly lit darkness, Rose could imagine how beautiful it all was in daylight.

She didn't usually stay after the lesson and join her students for the meal they had created, but Lucas had insisted and frankly, Rose thought with an inner sigh, she hadn't wanted to leave. Probably not a good idea to start getting attached, she warned herself sternly, but then she had always had a soft spot for Lucas King. She couldn't explain it. It just...*was*.

Still, after two hours of working closely together in his amazingly wonderful kitchen, Rose still couldn't have said that she knew Lucas any better than she once had. Oh, he seemed friendly enough, despite the thin thread of distance he insisted on keeping between them.

But then, she reminded herself as she looked back at her memories, Lucas had always been a little closed off. That's probably what had drawn her to him in the first place, Rose realized. In her own family, the men had been outgoing, gregarious. Whatever they were thinking, they didn't keep to themselves. They were loud and emotional and easy to read.

Meeting Lucas had been like brushing up against a gorgeous mystery. His blue eyes held secrets, his almost unreadable expressions tempted her to delve deeper and his quiet self-assurance had been a welcome difference from her brother and father.

He'd attracted her with his quiet thoughtfulness and, apparently, that hadn't changed.

"Earth to Rose," he said, snapping his fingers in front of her face.

She came up out of her thoughts fast and gave herself a shake. "Sorry. What?"

Lucas gave her a half smile. "You zoned out. Was it the sparkling conversation or the slightly charred chicken breast?"

She laughed a little. "The chicken is just a little well done," she said, glancing down at the salsa-covered meat on her plate. "Not bad at all for a first try."

"So the conversation put you to sleep?"

"No," she said, taking a bite of the mushroom au gratin casserole. "But the lack of it might. You haven't had a lot to say in the last hour or so, Lucas."

"Cooking takes concentration," he said with a shrug.

"Is that all it is?"

He looked at her. "What else would it be?"

"I don't know," she mused, taking a small sip of the chardonnay he had poured for both of them. "Maybe you're regretting hiring me? After the way you and Dave left things, I'm still not sure why you hired me in the first place."

His features tightened briefly at the mention of her brother, and, once again, Rose really wished she knew what had come between the two men. One day, their friendship was just…over. Lucas hadn't come around anymore, and Dave had refused to talk about it with her. Unfortunately, that hadn't changed two years later. Neither of them seemed willing to satisfy her curiosity.

"Dave's got nothing to do with this," Lucas murmured. "You teach cooking, I need to learn, end of story."

"If you say so." She didn't believe him. Sure, there had been the coincidence of him seeing her at his neighbor's house. But what had moved him to ask her to help him learn to cook? Why would he suddenly be willing to talk to the sister of the man he hadn't spoken to in years? There was more here and she'd eventually get to the bottom of it. But for now, she was willing to let it go.

"So what did you think of the mushrooms au gratin?"

He grinned and took a big bite of the casserole side dish in question. Once he'd chewed and swallowed, he said, "It proves that with enough sour cream and cheese, anything is edible. Even fungi and parsley."

"A lovely compliment," she said, chuckling. "But you have to admit, the first meal you cooked turned out pretty well."

"Better than Kathy Robertson's?"

"Why are men so competitive?"

"It's a gift. So?"

"Yes," she reluctantly admitted. "I don't really like to talk about my clients, but yours was way better. Kathy burned the onions so badly, I had to throw one of my favorite pans away."

He shuddered. "Hope she kept the name of the last caterer she used."

Laughing, Rose said, "That was just mean. She's going to get the hang of it."

He studied her for so long, Rose began to shift uneasily in her chair. "What?"

"Nothing," he said with a shake of his head. "But you

really are a positive, glass-is-half-full kind of woman, aren't you?"

Rose tensed briefly. For most of her life, she had pretty much been the Pollyanna type. She looked for the good around her and generally found it. Until, of course, her ex-husband had not only snatched off her rose-colored glasses, but also ground them to dust under his heel.

After that, she'd had to fight to regain her sense of well-being. She'd had to force herself to smile until, eventually, it had become real. And now, she wasn't going to go back to the dark side again. She wasn't going to apologize because she liked rainbows and puppies and laughing children.

"Seeing the empty half doesn't make you more mature or more intelligent," she said softly. "It only means you're looking for what you don't have. How is that a good thing?"

"I didn't mean—"

"It's okay," she said, folding her napkin and standing up. "I like a half-full glass. And if yours is half-empty, then I'm sorry."

He stiffened as if she'd hit a sore spot. Instantly, Rose regretted the fact that their semipleasant evening had deteriorated somehow. But maybe it was better this way. Keep the distance of teacher and student between them. Because he hadn't hired her to be his friend—or anything else. This was a job. A good-paying job at that, and she wasn't willing to risk it by opening up doors that should probably remain closed.

"My glass is just fine, thanks," he said, his voice hardly more than a low rumble of sound.

"Glad to hear it." Rose looked at him, and, in spite of knowing that she should just keep her mouth shut and protect this very well-paying job, she just had to say, "Maybe your glass is full, but if it's holding the wrong things, what difference does it make?"

"*What?*"

"Never mind. Dumb analogy anyway. Look, why don't I help you clean this up? Then we'll make out a menu and a grocery list for tomorrow."

She left him sitting at the table and even though she didn't look around, Rose knew he was still watching her when she started loading the dishwasher.

"That's it, you're paying my dues at Weight Watchers."

"Hmm?" Lucas looked up from the sheaf of papers he had been staring at for an hour without really reading any of it and looked at his secretary. "Evelyn, what're you talking about?"

"This." She held up an oversize frosted cookie and shook it at him. "Ever since Rafe married Katie, we've got these amazing cookies in the break room every day."

"That's a bad thing?" he asked, smiling.

Evelyn was in her late fifties with a rounded figure and short, graying brown hair. She was smart, efficient and knew as much as Lucas did about running crews and the customer base. She'd been with him for five years and had long since let go of her polite, businesslike tone with him.

"I've gained five pounds," she muttered and gave the cookie a glare before taking a bite and nearly groaning in pleasure.

"Don't eat them," he said with a shrug.

"Excellent advice," she muttered with a dark look. "Why didn't I think of that?"

"Evelyn, was there a point to this?"

She sighed in defeat, took another nibble of the

cookie and said, "There's trouble on the Johnson site. The crew started digging for the new gas line before the WeDig people came out to clear the site and they hit the water line."

"Perfect." Anger churned his guts. His crews were more professional than that. They knew damn well that any digging had to be cleared by the city guys who came out to tell them where gas, water and cable lines were, giving them specific areas to avoid. "Who's in charge of that site?"

She rolled her eyes. "Warren."

"Damn it."

"Exactly," Evelyn said. "He's on line two right now, wanting to talk to you."

"Good. I've got a few things to say to him, too." He waved one hand at his secretary, who backed out of his office chewing on her cookie and moaning like a woman having sex.

Oh, now there was an image he didn't need in his head. Evelyn. Having sex.

He snatched up the phone, pushed line two and snapped, "Warren, what the hell is going on? You dug before getting the go-ahead?"

"Not me, boss. It was Rick. The new guy. Got impatient, I guess. I was making a run to a supply shop for more pipe. When I got back, it was like the Great Flood out there."

"You're in charge, Warren," Lucas told him, tired of the man's excuses. Whenever anything went wrong on one of his sites, he was never around. Always off doing something else. "You give the orders on this project, and you take your orders from *me*. You damn well know better than to dig before WeDig comes out to clear it and the guys should know it, too."

"Yeah, but—"

"No more buts. I'll be at the site in a half hour. For now, get some pumps in there to clear the yard and get that water pipe capped off."

"Already done."

"That's something anyway…" Shaking his head, he added, "Keep the guys on site until I get there."

"Right, boss."

When he hung up, Lucas was still furious, but almost grateful for the shift in his thoughts. If not for Warren's ineptitude, he'd have nothing on his mind but Rose Clancy. And he'd already done nothing but think about her since the night before.

She had haunted his dreams, making sleep nearly impossible, and then this morning over his cup of coffee, he'd smelled her in his kitchen. It was as if she was imprinting herself on his consciousness.

Now, Lucas thought back to how Dave had always described his sister. Younger, softer, easily hurt and scared of her own shadow. She hadn't sounded all that appealing to him until the day he first met her. Then, her looks had bowled him over first and her laughter had hit him hard There was something about a woman who knew how to laugh, he thought now. Maybe it was because growing up, he'd never heard his own mother laugh at a damn thing. Whining on the other hand… she had been very good at that.

As soon as that thought entered his mind, Lucas deliberately shut it down. It had sounded bad—disloyal—even to himself. His mom had done the best she could. She had just been too…alone.

Hell. Memories from his childhood weren't going to make this situation any easier to deal with. Disgusted with himself and his lack of concentration, Lucas pushed aside all thoughts but those related to work. For most of his life, work had been his sanctuary. The place in the world where everything was as it should be. Where the rules were well-defined and always followed. Here, Lucas kept his finger on the pulse of the company. Here, he wasn't questioned, just obeyed. Here, he was—

"How'd it go last night?"

"What?" He looked up as Sean strolled into his office and plopped himself down into one of the three chairs in front of Lucas's desk. He was chewing on one of the frosted cookies.

"Did you know we've got cookies in the break room now?" He held one hand to his heart and bowed his head. "Thank you, sister Katie...."

"Yeah, I heard," Lucas muttered. "Apparently a Weight Watchers class is in the offing."

"Not for me," Sean said with a laugh as he licked the last bit of frosting from his finger.

Lucas sighed. "Is there a reason you're here?"

"Yep. Curiosity. How did it go last night? You know. With Rose?"

"How did you know about that?"

"Your secretary told my secretary, who told me and…" He shrugged and grinned. "Here I am. Seriously? Cooking lessons?"

Frowning, Lucas leafed through a pile of papers on his desk. He didn't want to talk about this with Sean. Hadn't he just been focusing on *not* thinking about her? For all the good it had done him.

In spite of his best efforts, she kept popping back into his mind. Her smile. The way light flashed on her long blond hair. The sound of her laugh and the fresh, lemony scent of her. It was all right there whether he wanted it to be or not.

"Nothing to say?" Sean whistled low and long. "Must be even more interesting than I figured."

Glaring at his brother, Lucas demanded, "Don't you have something to do?"

"Actually, yeah. I'm headed out to look into a new service provider. With the way the company's expanding, our old one just isn't keeping up."

Lucas didn't even have to pretend disinterest Sean was enamored of all the technological aspects of the business, but once he started talking about it, Lucas's eyes glazed over. "Good," he said. "Go do it."

"In a sec." Sean leaned forward, bracing his elbows on his knees. "So tell me."

"Tell you what?" He dropped the papers on his desk and sighed as he figured the fastest way to get rid of his brother was to answer his questions. "You already know I hired her."

Sean laughed. "For cooking lessons."

"Why is that so hard to understand?"

"Seriously?" Sean shook his head and stood up. "*You,* cooking? I should have been more impressed with her. Blonde, beautiful and a miracle worker. Teaching *you* to cook? Does she get hazard pay?"

Frowning, Lucas thought of the triple-her-usual-salary offer he'd made and realized that she *was* getting hazard pay. His scowl deepened as he snapped, "I've cooked for you before and you're still breathing."

"Only because of my excellent digestive system. It can withstand all sorts of toxins."

"Get out, Sean."

"Going, Lucas," he said amiably.

"Oh—" Lucas stopped him with a single word. "There's trouble at the Johnson site."

"Warren again?" Sean frowned.

"Yeah, they dug without the okay and hit a water pipe. Apparently the home owner can now dock a boat off the patio."

Shaking his head, Sean said, "I know the crews are your department, but if you want my opinion, we ought to get rid of Warren. We spend more time cleaning up after him than anything else. He's more trouble than he's worth."

"Agreed." Lucas nodded. "We'll talk about it at the weekly meeting."

"Right." Sean headed for the door, but before he left, he asked, "On the Rose front, I hope cooking lessons are all you're really up to."

"What?"

"I hope you're not still planning on using her for payback on Dave. Because, my man, that way lies misery."

Lucas didn't say anything, just stared at his younger brother until Sean shrugged and walked out. But long after he was gone, the man's words were still ringing in the air.

Was he right? Was Lucas just asking for trouble by using Rose to get back at Dave?

Standing up, he turned his back on the work waiting for him and stared out the window at the world beyond the glass. Long Beach was shivering under gray skies and a cold rain driven by an icy ocean wind. Oak trees rattled bare limbs, and the tall pines swayed with each gust.

Truth be told, Lucas didn't much like the idea of using Rose, either, though damned if he'd admit that to Sean. But the bottom line was, she was the sister of a man who had cheated him. Lied to him. And Lucas couldn't let that slide.

Liars deserved what they got, he told himself as his hands fisted at his sides. Hadn't he grown up watching his mother's heart broken again and again by the very men she had trusted to keep her safe? First, it was his father, Ben King—though to give Ben his due, he hadn't promised Lucas's mother any more than he had the mothers of any of his sons.

But Lucas's mother had pinned her hopes on love. Time and again, she'd gone searching for it, only to have whatever man she was pining over use her up and let her go. Her trust shaken, her heart shattered more times than he could even count, she'd finally given up. Destroyed by the very emotion she'd so longed to feel.

No, betrayal couldn't be forgiven. Or forgotten. And he'd do whatever he had to do to make sure that Dave Clancy finally understood that.

Three

"How's Rafe doing?"

"What?"

As Rose followed him down the wide aisle in the grocery store, Lucas heard her sigh heavily. "Your brother? Rafe? Didn't he get married a few months ago?"

"Oh. Yeah. He did." Lucas frowned at the seemingly endless selection of products. He'd spent most of his life avoiding grocery stores. When he needed food in a hurry, he stopped in at a deli or something. He hadn't been raised around a kitchen and, as a King, if he wanted someone cooking in his house, he could hire a damn chef. So why learn?

Now, he felt like a stranger in a strange land. The brilliant fluorescent lighting gave him a headache. There was a screaming child a few aisles over and an old woman had just crashed her cart into his and then had the guts to blame *him*. Seriously, men just didn't belong in grocery stores.

He was actually starting to rethink his whole plan. He hadn't really considered at the beginning just what all this would entail. And his interest in cooking was about as low as it could get. Then he reminded himself sternly that getting back at Dave would be worth all the hassles he was going through at the moment. Nobody betrayed a King and walked away.

Nobody.

"And?" Rose prompted. "How's he doing?"

"Rafe?" He dragged his mind back to the conversation. "He's good. Seems happy enough."

"What a touching testimony for marriage," she mused and reached over to pick up a box of bread crumbs.

"Bread crumbs aren't on the list," Lucas said, checking just to make sure.

"I know, but it's good to have them in the house. They come in handy in all kinds of ways. These are the best," she said, handing him the blue box. "Low in sodium and carbs, plus they're crispier than ordinary bread crumbs."

"Crispier is better. Right." If he did inadvertently learn how to cook during this process, he promised himself, he'd hire somebody to shop for him.

"So, you don't like Rafe's wife?"

He blinked at her. "Where did that come from? Of course I like her."

"Well, you don't seem thrilled that he got married," she said with a shrug. "So I assumed you didn't like his wife."

"So if I didn't like Christmas that would mean I hated somebody else's present?" What was it with women? A man makes a simple statement and they take it and run in the exact opposite direction.

"You don't like Christmas?" she countered.

"I didn't say that." Shaking his head, he continued down the baking aisle. "Have you ever heard the word *logic?*"

"I don't know," she said on a laugh. "I may have heard a vague reference at some point. Sounds like Latin."

"Naturally," he muttered, ignoring her smile, because frankly he didn't like the buzz of interest he felt lighting up his insides. He had a plan here, and he wasn't about to be distracted from it. Yes, he was going to seduce her. But that didn't mean he was going to do something stupid like come to care for her.

Keeping his voice lighter than the tension filling him would ordinarily warrant, he said, "I like Katie fine. She's way too good for Rafe, if you ask me."

"So it's just marriage in general you're against?"

"Pretty much." He stopped dead, and she crashed into him.

"Sorry."

He ignored the increased buzzing in his blood and told himself to get a grip on the situation. To get his mind off what his body was clamoring for, he scanned the shelves of spices and was instantly irritated. "How can there be so many?"

"Ah," she said with an understanding grin, "life outside the narrow confines of garlic, salt and pepper."

He frowned. "Nothing wrong with salt and pepper. It's basic. Classic."

"Boring."

"Fine," he said. Anything to get out of here that much sooner. "What do we need? I mean, what do *I* need?"

"It's all there on the list," she urged and stood by, deliberately letting him find his way through the spice racks.

He squinted at labels and hissed at the elevated prices of some of the more esoteric spices. Who knew this stuff was so expensive? Thoughts rolled through his mind even as he continued to read labels. The Kings should look into this. If they could set up suppliers, they could move into the spice industry and really take it over. *King Spice,* he thought with a half smile. It could work.

Now here was where he felt comfortable, Lucas thought. Planning, focusing on business and growing the ever-expanding King empire. Get him the hell out of a grocery store and there was nothing that could stop him once his mind was set on something. He slid a glance in Rose's direction. Her big blue eyes were fixed on him, a quiet smile tugging at her lips. Even in this hideous lighting, her skin was like porcelain and the long ponytail she habitually wore spilled across one shoulder, her thick blond hair a tempting mass of waves and loose curls.

She was enough to make any red-blooded male take a long, second look. Hell, he'd looked plenty himself when he had first met her. But Dave had practically wrapped her up in barbed wire and posted a No Trespassing sign over her head. So Lucas had kept his distance out of respect for his friend.

That respect was long dead, though, and soon he'd have this luscious-looking woman right where he wanted her. In his bed. *Under him.*

Until then, he'd just focus on the task at hand, he told himself, as he shifted his gaze back to the damned racks of spices.

* * *

Rose couldn't seem to tear her gaze off of Lucas. His black leather jacket was open to reveal the plain white T-shirt beneath. Black jeans clung to his long, muscular legs and he was wearing the same scuffed boots she had noticed the day before. What was it, she wondered, about a gorgeous man in jeans and cowboy boots? Was it instinctive? Did it pull at something primal in a woman?

Or was it simply that Lucas King would look too good in absolutely anything? Sadly, she thought, the latter was probably closer to the truth.

"I don't see peppercorns," he muttered, "and why can't I just use ground-up pepper? Why do I have to grind it myself? Haven't we come further than that as a society?"

"Funny," she said and reached out to tap one fingernail against the peppercorns. Right in front of him. Somehow, she found that thought comforting. Lucas was so…formidable, that finding out he was like other men in the can't-find-something-directly-in-front-of-him way made him seem…not ordinary by any means. But more *touchable*.

Not that she was thinking about touching him. All right, she was. But what woman wouldn't when she was standing right beside Lucas King? Still, if there was one thing Rose had learned in the last year or so, it was that she didn't want anything to do with another alpha male.

Lucas picked up the bottle of peppercorns, tossed it into the cart then consulted his list again. "Kosher salt? I'm not Jewish. You know that, right?"

Was he trying to be charming, she wondered, or was it just part of who he was? And if he was trying, *why?* Three years ago, when they first met, he had never made a move on her. And back then, she would definitely have been interested.

"Kosher salt is pure," she said, still studying him, trying to figure him out. "No chemicals. It's better for you."

"Fine."

"So why do you hate marriage?" she asked, returning to their earlier conversation.

"Didn't say I hated it," he told her, not even bothering to glance her way.

"Really didn't have to," she pointed out.

"Why are you such a fan?" He straightened up, turned his head and gave her a flat stare. "Didn't you get divorced yourself only last year?"

His eyes were sharp and cool and distant. There was accusation in their depths, and she frowned to herself at the justice in it. He was right, after all. She wasn't exactly a stellar example of a good marriage. "Fine, you're right. I did get divorced last year. But how did you know about it? You and Dave never talk and oh... never mind. Gossip columns. I know I made all the papers and even a few of the tabloids when I divorced Henry."

"Please. I don't read that crap. But word does get around." He looked at her for a moment or two longer before he said, "Never did understand why you married that guy in the first place, if you don't mind my saying."

"Nope, don't mind," she said with a sigh. Henry Porter had been a mistake from the jump. But the real mistake had been in allowing her father and brother to talk her into marrying the jerk for the sake of the family. Henry's business had aligned nicely with theirs, since he was an architect with a string of successful upscale housing developments in his portfolio. Dave had figured that by working with Porter's Palaces—idiotic name for a company, in Rose's opinion—Clancy Construction would take the next step up the proverbial ladder.

Of course, then her father died, Henry showed his true colors and Rose had reclaimed her life, leaving Dave fuming.

"So?" he asked again, his voice quiet beneath the Muzak constantly pumped through the store. "Why'd you do it? And don't try to tell me you actually loved that pompous twit Porter."

"No," she said with a rueful smile. "That's one mistake I didn't make."

When she didn't elaborate further, Lucas shrugged and grabbed a tiny plastic jar of cloves. He tossed it into the cart before searching for the next one on his list. "Don't want to talk about it?"

"Not particularly," she admitted.

She knew all too well what he'd heard about the end of her marriage. Rose shifted uncomfortably, remembering the humiliation of her marriage and the horrific ending of it. She'd married the wrong man for all the wrong reasons. She'd gone along with her family because that's who she had always been.

The pleaser. That was Rose. Always going out of her way to make sure everyone around her was happy. She'd subjugated her own wants and needs in favor of everyone else's. Well, those days were gone. She'd learned her lesson the hard way, but now, she was determined to make *herself* happy.

He tore his gaze away from the spice shelf and shot a quick look at her. If she hadn't known better, she would have thought she saw a quick flash of regret in his eyes. But it was gone almost immediately, so she dismissed it as a trick of the overhead lights. "I didn't mean—"

"Sure you did," Rose interrupted, then pointed. "There's the rosemary. Get the big bottle."

As he did, she watched him. "You wanted to point out that I was being a sunshine-and-rainbow girl with nothing to back it up."

He nodded, then turned his head to look at her. His black hair fell across his forehead and his eyes narrowed on her. "I suppose I did."

"Thanks for admitting it, anyway," she told him. "And you're right. I absolutely don't have any personal experience with a happy marriage." Reaching out, she picked up a box of blueberry muffin mix, read the back and wrinkled her nose before setting it back down. "Look, my marriage was a disaster, but I went into it for all the wrong reasons—"

"What were they?"

She looked at him. "None of your business. The point is," she continued, "just because my marriage didn't work, doesn't mean there's something wrong with the whole institution."

"Institution," he muttered. "That word says it all."

"Is that how Rafe sees it?"

He laughed shortly, checked his list again and glanced at her. The amusement in his eyes was real this time and the curve of his lips did something amazing to the pit of her stomach. "He's too crazy about Katie to think anything at this point. And my brother Sean is ecstatic because now he's related to the cookie queen and has all kinds of expectations for free food."

"What about you? Any expectations?"

He stilled, looked her up and down and, in that blink of time, Rose felt her skin begin to hum and sizzle. "Not where Katie's concerned, no."

They had really veered into what could quickly

become uncomfortable territory. Funny, to be having such a deep conversation in the middle of the baking aisle, with Muzak pouring down from overhead and a child still screaming in fury somewhere in the distance.

Seconds ticked past and neither of them looked away. Rose felt the searing heat of his gaze licking at her skin and in another minute or two, she might just melt into a puddle.

Thankfully, she was spared that humiliation when Lucas spoke up.

"I've got all the spices. What's next?"

Spices. Spicy. Sexy. Sex...

"What? Oh. Right." She shook her head hard, ridding herself of the images rushing through her mind. Images of Lucas, bending down, kissing her, holding her, leaning her back onto a bed and... "First we'll get some olive oil, then we'll head to the butcher department."

She walked farther down the aisle, silently lecturing herself about hormonal surges and inappropriate behavior with a client and anything else she could think of to take her mind off of Lucas. Naked.

God.

He followed behind her with the cart and stopped when she did. Staring at the long shelf crowded with dozens of types of oils, Lucas looked about as lost as a man could get. "Why do we need so many different kinds of oil? How're you supposed to know what to get?"

"Always get the extra virgin," she said.

His eyebrows lifted and his mouth quirked. "There's *extra* virgin?"

He was amused again. Perfect. She was simmering, he was chuckling. Oh, this was going just fabulously well.

"Just get this one," she said and reached for a bottle on the top shelf.

He went for it at the same time and their hands brushed over the heavy plastic bottle. That one instant of contact was all she needed to kick that smoldering fire inside her into an inferno. Rose was really tempted to take him down the ice cream aisle. At least there, the frigid air might do something to help quash the heat threatening to engulf her. Instead, she led him to the butcher department and tried to keep her mind on cuts of beef and pork loins.

A half hour later, they were finishing up in the produce section. Lucas couldn't have been less interested as she explained what to look for in fresh broccoli. "You want dark green florets and thinnish stalks."

"Thinnish?"

"Yes. Not too skinny, not too fat."

His gaze raked her up and down again, and Rose had to take a deep breath. She was beginning to think he was deliberately trying to get her all jangled up. He was making her nervous and clearly enjoying himself at the same time.

"You know, not *everything* I say is intended as a come-on of some kind."

"Just a happy accident, then?" he inquired.

"Lucas?" A high-pitched, completely surprised feminine voice stopped whatever Rose might have said in return. Instead, she turned to watch a voluptuous redhead in skin-tight jeans and three-inch black heels scurrying toward them, a beaming smile on her gorgeous face. The woman was made up as if she were going to an opera. Yet, she had a small basket tucked over her arm, the single tomato and avocado inside rolling from one side to the other in her agitation.

"Marsha," Lucas said stiffly. "Nice to see you."

The words were right, Rose thought, but the tone in his voice should have warned the redhead off.

"I can't believe you're in a grocery store, of all places," the redhead crooned, leaning in to brush an air kiss in the vicinity of his cheek.

Rose took a step backward, sliding away to give the two of them a minute alone. Maybe Lucas didn't seem happy about running into the woman, but she doubted that Marsha would miss her presence. Rose had every intention of hiding behind the bin of Vidalia onions, but Lucas stopped her cold with one hand on her arm. His grip tightened as she tried to squirm free, but the redhead never noticed. Her big green eyes were fixed on Lucas as if he were a Prada bag on a seventy-five-percent-off table.

"Imagine, running into you here, of all places."

"Yeah," he said, "you said that already. Not really surprising, Marsha, I do eat."

"Yes," she agreed on a seductive chuckle, "but you forget, I've seen your refrigerator for myself."

Perfect, Rose thought. Nothing like standing here witnessing one of Lucas's bedmates trying to metaphorically lick him in the produce aisle. And could she have looked any more hideous, Rose wondered furiously. Why was her hair in a ponytail, of all things? And why hadn't she worn her *new* jeans...instead of her favorite, often-washed, faded pair?

And *why,* she demanded silently, did she *care?*

She wasn't on a date, for heaven's sake. She and Lucas weren't a couple. He was a client. A customer. She was his cooking teacher, nothing more.

Which should have made her feel better but it *so* didn't.

"You look wonderful, Lucas," Marsha said, her voice dropping to a low purr of interest.

Behind Lucas, Rose rolled her eyes and willed herself to sink into the floor. Nothing happened.

"Thanks, you, too," Lucas said brusquely. Then he added, "You'll have to excuse us, though, we've got to finish shopping and get home."

"We?" For the first time, Marsha's gaze slid past Lucas to notice Rose. Surprise flickered across her eyes briefly.

"Marsha Hancock, this is Rose Clancy. Rose, Marsha."

"Hi. Nice to meet you," Rose said when she couldn't avoid it.

"Uh-huh," Marsha murmured, then turned her renewed interest on Lucas. "Like I was saying, you look wonderful and if you're not busy this Friday, I'm having a small, intimate party at my place and—"

"We'll be busy," Lucas told her, then looked at Rose. "What do you think, honey, we done here?"

Honey? He'd called her *honey?* Rose's mouth opened and closed a few times while she tried to think of something clever—heck, *anything* to say. Then Lucas dropped one arm around her shoulders and gave her a hard hug. Keeping her tucked in close to his side, he looked at the redhead and said, "Yep, guess we're done. Good seeing you, Marsha."

He pushed the laden cart one-handed, still keeping one arm draped around Rose. She walked right beside him, trying to figure out what had just happened. Risking a quick glance backward, she could see that the beautiful Marsha was trying to understand the same thing.

Rose stood beside him while he paid for the groceries,

then followed him out to the parking lot and his car when he was finished. A cold night wind blew in off the ocean, and, overhead, the stars were glittering.

She turned her face into the wind as he loaded up the trunk of his SUV and didn't say a word until he'd finished and closed the lid again with a solid *thunk*.

"What was that about? Inside there, with Marsha?"

He shrugged, and pushed the shopping cart into the area set aside for them. "Marsha's annoying. Letting her believe you and I were together was the easiest way of getting rid of her."

He might think she was annoying now, but the redhead had made it all too clear that at one point in the not so distant past, Lucas had found her much more interesting.

"And you had to call me 'honey' to get that point across?"

"Seemed like a good idea at the time." He tilted his head and looked at her as one corner of his mouth turned up. He took a few steps closer and with every step, he asked, "You object to 'honey'? How about 'babe'? 'Darlin'? 'Sweetie'?"

Her insides were shaking, and her mouth was dry. Rose looked up into those blue eyes of his and couldn't read what he was thinking. Not enough lights in this parking lot. Too many shadows in his eyes, on his features.

"But I'm not any of those things to you, Lucas," she pointed out and backed up until she bumped into his SUV. "What if she starts telling people that she saw us together? That you called me 'honey'? That we looked like a couple?"

"That would be bad?" he asked.

"It wouldn't be honest."

"And you're always honest."

"Try to be."

"Fine," he said, leaning into her and bracing both hands on his car at either side of her, "answer me this, then. And try to be honest. What would you do right now if I kissed you?"

Her knees went weak.

This was just ridiculous.

She was a grown woman. A divorced woman. She was no shy virgin sighing with eagerness because the captain of the football team happened to notice she was alive.

She was still looking up into his eyes, and he was still waiting for an answer to his question. His scent swirled around her, something spicy and all too male. His face was just a breath away from hers. The heat of his body seeped into hers and she felt that smoldering fire inside her erupt into something a lot more volcanic.

Rose had a choice here. She could be completely professional, and tell him that she didn't want him to kiss her. But that would be a big, fat lie. *Or,* she could be honest and tell him that if he kissed her, she'd probably explode with all of the banked sexual energy she was feeling at the moment.

So what was it going to be?

He licked his lips and just like that, her decision was made. Three years ago, when she had first met him, she'd daydreamed about being kissed by Lucas King.

Now, she was about to find out if her fantasies were as good as the reality.

"Well, Rose?"

"You want honest?" she asked.

"Yeah."

"Okay then." She grabbed the lapels of his black leather jacket and yanked him down to her.

His mouth closed over hers and what felt like an electrical charge blasted them both.

Rose wrapped her arms around his neck and held on while his tongue parted her lips and slipped into the heat of her mouth. She sighed into him and instantly tangled her tongue with his, as eager and hungry for him as he seemed to be for her.

Her stomach flipped, her heartbeat staggered in heavy beats and the knees that had been weak before turned to water under the onslaught of too many sensations to count.

He pulled her close, pressing her to his length, and she felt every hard, muscled inch of him imprinting itself on her body. A throbbing ache settled between her thighs as he swept his hands up and down her back, caressing her behind.

She couldn't breathe. Could hardly stand.

But at least, she thought idly, she had her answer.

The reality of kissing Lucas King was *way* better than the fantasy.

Four

Lucas was hanging on to his common sense by a quickly unraveling thread.

She felt so...*good* in his arms. He hadn't expected that. Hadn't expected her taste to enflame him or for the scent of lemons that clung to her to drive into his mind and cloud up his thoughts. The feel of her body pressed against his only made him harder. He pulled her closer, to let her know what he was feeling, and when she moaned, it almost pushed him over the edge and down a very slippery slope.

He had thought time would have muted the attraction that drew him to her. But it hadn't. One taste and all he could think was...he wanted more.

One kiss, that's all this was supposed to have been. A small preview of things to come. To get her thinking about him. Dreaming about him.

But it was so much more.

Rose Clancy.

Her name lit up in his mind like a shock of neon and that was enough to have him ending the kiss, however reluctantly. Lucas pulled away, though his every instinct clamored at him to hold her even tighter. He took one long breath and then another, hoping to steady himself.

This wasn't the time for instincts. Or urges. This was a time for logic and cool thinking, and damned if he'd risk his plan by seducing her in the parking lot of a damn grocery store.

Somewhere close by, a car's engine fired up, and Lucas took a step back from her, deliberately putting some distance between them. He could still taste her. Feel her.

Shoving one hand through his hair, Lucas thought that maybe Sean had been right. It *had* been too long since he'd been with a woman. That's why Rose had gotten to him so completely. Hell, he was practically a starving man. Was it any wonder that a tender steak looked good to him?

His gaze was locked on her. She leaned against his car, lifting one hand to her mouth and holding the other hand up as if to warn him to stay away. Not really necessary, Lucas thought, but he got the message.

She was as shaken as he.

And that was a good thing, he told himself. At least he knew now that she would be thinking about him. Remembering this kiss, just as—he hated to admit it— he would.

"That was—"

"Rose—"

"—not something that's going to happen again," she finished, surprising him.

She straightened up, smoothed her hair and took

another breath. After a second or two, she met his eyes and gave him a smile that was so forced it was more of a grimace.

"I can't say I didn't enjoy it, but Lucas, you should know that I'm not looking for a relationship."

Stunned, he could only stare at her. *She* was giving *him* the don't-expect-anything-from-me speech? Had the world gone completely crazy? Her eyes were soft, her expression kind but remote, and Lucas was at a loss for something to say. This kind of thing didn't happen to him.

Women didn't turn away from Lucas King. They generally chased him down and did whatever they could to hang on to him.

"Excuse me?" he finally managed to say.

"Look, I'm sorry. I should have said something the minute I agreed to work for you." She inhaled and rushed on before he could speak. "I noticed right away that there was an...*attraction* between us, but I didn't think anything of it. It's my own fault, I should have said something sooner. But the truth is, I'm not looking for another man in my life—"

She wasn't—

"I don't remember offering," he said, his voice tightly controlled. Anger and disbelief warred in the pit of his stomach, kicking up an ugly brew as he felt the sting of rejection for the first time in his life.

She ignored that jibe. "And if I were considering getting involved with someone," Rose continued, "it wouldn't be with you."

Completely shocked now, he just stared at her, too amazed to speak for a moment. This was not how he'd seen this little chat going. He'd expected to have to talk her down from their passionate kiss. To ease her gently into the seduction he had planned. What he *hadn't* counted on was being insulted.

"What do you mean it wouldn't be me? What the hell is wrong with *me?*" he finally shouted.

Rose winced and looked past him at the brightly lit grocery store as if checking to make sure no one else had come out and was listening.

Then she turned her gaze back to him. "Nothing's wrong with you, Lucas. You're just…not my type."

"Type?" he echoed. This was not happening, he told himself sternly. No way was he standing in a grocery store parking lot looking at a beautiful woman and hearing her tell him to buzz off. This was so far out of his universe, he didn't have a clue how to handle it. But his temper was on the rise and a sudden, pounding headache erupted behind his eyes.

Crossing his arms over his chest, he glared at her. "What type am I then?"

"Bossy."

"Bossy isn't a type," he argued, because he couldn't argue with the word itself. Sure he was bossy, but he preferred to think of that trait as confidence. All of the Kings were confident in themselves and their abilities, and they didn't suffer fools, either. They took charge, got things done and steamrolled over whomever might be dumb enough to stand in their way.

Lucas was no different.

Yeah, he'd been called arrogant before. And unrelenting. And even, on occasion, egotistical. But it was a small price to pay for getting what he wanted when he wanted it. And he wasn't about to apologize to Rose Clancy—or anyone else for that matter—for being the man he was.

"Just when exactly have I bossed you around?" he challenged, his eyes locked with hers.

She sighed. "You haven't, in so many words. Not yet, anyway."

"Oh, so you're a fortune teller, too? You can read the future and so you know I'm going to start giving you orders?"

"I don't need to read the future," she told him, stiffening her spine and lifting her chin in defense against his tone. "All I have to do is look at the past."

"That makes no sense, either," he told her.

"It does to me," she said simply.

Lucas shook his head and tried to rein in the million and one thoughts churning through his mind. Then he gave it up. How could he find logic in what was unreasonable to begin with? Was his plan for revenge going to end right here, beneath a flickering, ready-to-burn-out parking light?

"I can't believe any of this," he muttered, more to himself than to her.

"I know. You probably don't hear it often."

His eyes narrowed. "Try never."

She winced. "I am sorry, but Lucas, I really need this job and I don't want us to work together under false pretenses."

A part of him relaxed a little. She wasn't walking away at least. She was just trying to put him on notice. "Uh-huh."

"That kiss notwithstanding, I really think we should just keep our relationship to teacher and student. Okay?"

Man, he thought, if Sean were here listening to this, his brother would be laughing his ass off. Hell, if it were happening to one of his brothers, Lucas would be doing the same thing. But it was damned hard to see the humor in the situation from his perspective.

On the other hand, Lucas mused as he watched her, Rose was the one to initiate that steam-inducing kiss—and she would have kept on kissing him if he hadn't called a halt and taken a step back. Say what she wanted now, he had tasted her desire, felt her need wrapping itself around him. Rose Clancy wanted him as much as he wanted her—which would only work in his favor as he went about seducing her. Good to know that beneath her cool, prim, good-girl demeanor, she was burning with the same fire that was licking at his insides.

So…fine. He'd play along. Let her think she was in charge. Eventually, the game would shift in his favor.

Things always did.

She was watching him warily, waiting for his response, and damned if he wasn't tempted to tell her to take her rules and get lost. He'd never before had a woman turn on him like this, especially after a kiss so hot—his lips still felt burned. And swallowing her "rules" was going to be hard to do, he knew. Yet, if he wanted his plan to work—and he really did—then he was going to have to go along with her…at least for now.

It grated, though, Lucas thought, as irritation spiked within him. He wasn't used to sublimating his own wants to anyone else's and if this is what it felt like, he had no interest in getting any better at it.

He looked at her and wanted her. He looked at her and wanted to turn and walk away. He looked at her and remembered her brother stabbing him and the rest of the Kings in the back and knew without a doubt that he wasn't willing to give up on his plan. Not yet.

So he'd go along. He'd let her think she had won this round, because winning a battle didn't mean winning the war. When this was over, it would be Lucas standing up and taking a bow. And it was that thought alone that had him nodding.

"Fine," he growled. "We'll do this your way."

She blew out a breath and flashed him a grin. "That's great. You'll see, Lucas. This will all work much better now that we both know the rules."

He watched her go to the passenger-side door and climb inside the already unlocked car. Alone in the flickering light of that lamp, Lucas clenched his jaw and promised himself that when this seduction ran its course and his payback had been achieved, *he* would be the one giving the not-my-type speech to Rose.

That realization had him smiling all the way home.

A week later, Rose was working on her home computer. This was her least favorite part of being self-employed. Well, there were also the quarterly tax reports. Frankly, anything to do with paperwork made her want to lie down on the couch until the resulting headache went away.

She loved cooking. Loved teaching others to do what she did best. But making what she loved a business demanded that she do a lot of what she hated, too.

Studying the spreadsheet across her computer screen, though, she had to smile. Thanks to Lucas King and the ridiculous amount of money he was willing to pay for cooking lessons, her bottom line was looking perceptibly better these days.

And her nerves were looking a lot worse, she acknowledged sadly. Picking up the mug in front of her, Rose took a long drink of her coffee and nearly gagged when she realized it had gone stone-cold. Grimacing at the taste, she carried the cup into the kitchen, saw the coffeepot was empty and automatically set it up to brew a fresh pot.

While the coffeemaker steamed and hissed and dripped, she leaned against her countertop and let her mind go to where, lately, it spent so much time.

Straight to Lucas.

In seconds, she was reliving that kiss again, as she had so many times over the last week. *What* had she been thinking? She should have edged away. Made an excuse. Laughed the tension off. But no, she'd had to grab his jacket lapels and drag him down for a kiss that was still reverberating through her seven days later.

"God, you're an idiot," she muttered, slapping one hand against the cool, gleaming surface of her cream-colored granite countertop.

She could still feel the hard thump of her heartbeat and the waves of desire that had crashed over her, nearly swamping her with a sense of need more desperate than she'd ever known before. Shaking her head, Rose absently reached for a dishtowel and dried and put away the few dishes sitting in the sink drainer while her mind taunted her by playing the memory of that kiss on a nonstop loop.

When she tired of torturing herself, she moved past that kiss and on to the strained conversation that had followed. She'd had to force herself to say what she had and heaven knew he hadn't taken it well.

"But then," she murmured, "why would he? No woman in her right mind would be pushing Lucas King away. No wonder he looked at me like I'd lost my mind."

Maybe she had, at that. She considered the suggestion objectively. She was single. Unattached. Clearly drawn to Lucas and his kiss had practically curled her toes and she had still turned him down. "Yep. Crazy."

When the phone rang, she jumped, then had to slap one hand to her chest to hold her heart in place. Shaking her head, she reached across the counter, and checked the caller ID. Smiling, she answered it.

"Dee, hi."

"I hate caller ID," her best friend said. "There are too few surprises in life anyway. Answering the phone should be like biting into a chocolate. A lottery, sort of. Will you get caramel or fruit and nuts?"

"Speaking of nuts," Rose said, still smiling, "what's going on?"

"Seriously?" Delilah James laughed and it was a deep, rumbling chuckle. "I'm calling for a passion update, of course."

"There is no update, and I'm sorry I ever told you about that kiss," Rose said, staring at the coffeemaker as if willing it to finish already. She'd need a lot more caffeine to deal with her best friend.

Delilah and Rose had met as roommates their freshman year of college and had bonded like sisters before the end of the first month of school. With similar backgrounds—each of them having been raised by wealthy, domineering fathers—they'd had a lot in common. The only difference being that at college, Dee had found the strength to stand up to her family's demands, while Rose hadn't.

"Of course, you're going to tell me about a kiss that fried all of your circuits," Dee said now. "I'm the best friend. Who else are you going to tell?"

"Nobody," she said and gratefully poured a fresh cup of coffee. "Honestly, it didn't mean anything."

"Right. That's why you were still babbling a day later. Why you said that you'd never experienced anything like that *and* it's why you said Lucas King kisses like a man who was just giving a woman a preview of the big event."

Rose closed her eyes on a sigh. "Did you take notes or something?"

"Are you kidding? I'm so jealous that description is seared into my mind." She gave a wistful, dramatic sigh. "So, what's the second chapter? Fondling in the kitchen? Playing touchy-feely while chopping parsley?"

"No to all of the above," Rose told her firmly, though her body did a quick hop and skip at the thought.

"You mean to tell me you're sticking to the rules you laid down? Strictly business?"

"I am," she said with a sharp nod that Dee couldn't even see. "I have to. I need the money he's paying me."

Dee snorted. "Oh, please."

Rose took the phone away from her ear, frowned at it, then slapped it back into place. "That's the reason I took the job in the first place, remember?"

"That's what you told yourself, anyway," Dee said. "Come on, Rose. We both know that Lucas King makes you shiver in all the right places."

True, she thought, rolling her eyes heavenward as she took a sip of hot coffee. Rose had been shivering for a solid week. And working in the man's house every night, in very close quarters, wasn't helping anything. Although, ever since that one, blistering kiss, Lucas had been absolutely, rigidly, polite. He hadn't made another move. Hadn't even so much as given her a look that would lead her to think that he'd spent nearly as much time daydreaming about that kiss as she had.

So *why* was she making herself crazy over this?

"Okay, yes, he does," she admitted, when Dee's silence began to scream at her. "But that doesn't mean I'm going to do anything about it."

"Pity."

"I'm sorry?"

"Rose, you know I love you…"

"I hear a *but* coming," Rose said.

"But," Dee continued, "you don't know a good thing when you trip over it."

"Oh, yes, I do," she countered, wandering across her small kitchen to stare out the window at the winterized backyard. The trees were looking a little sad, their browning leaves clinging to the branches, refusing to drop. The grass was brown, too. In fact, the only splotches of color out there were her chrysanthemums—yellow, purple, white—in the flowerbeds that needed weeding.

She'd lived in this house since her divorce, and she'd been happy here. Her own space, just a tiny bungalow in one of the older sections of Long Beach, the house was nothing like the palatial mansion where she'd grown up and, frankly, that was Rose's favorite part. Big houses felt cold. Empty.

Well, she amended silently, that wasn't entirely true. Lucas's house was gigantic, but there was an easy warmth to it, too. She had felt at home the moment she walked inside. Which probably wasn't a good thing.

"If you did," Dee was saying, "you'd kiss Lucas King senseless, tip him into bed and have your wicked way with him."

"You're writing your romance novel again, aren't you?"

Dee laughed. "Guilty. But my point is, why are you backing away? He's single. You're single. Finally."

"You know why," Rose said and opened the back door. It was cold outside, but right now, that sharp, ocean air felt good. As if it was going to blow right through her mind, chasing away thoughts she had no business indulging in.

Stepping out onto the back porch, Rose cradled the phone in one hand, her coffee cup in the other, and slowly sank down onto one of the weathered Adirondack chairs. Easing back, she stared into the yard, but wasn't really seeing it. Instead, she looked into her own past and didn't like the view.

"He's too much like Dave. And my father. And Henry," Rose said quietly.

"Rich men aren't all alike, sweetie," Dee said, her voice just as quiet, letting Rose know that she understood completely.

"No, but there are enough similarities between the Clancy men and the King men to make me wary."

"Okay, I get that," her friend said. "But you're not the same person you were in the past, Rose. There's not a man alive who could walk over you now. You're stronger than that. Not afraid to speak up for yourself."

She was, Rose thought with not a little pride. She'd worked hard to develop her own confidence. Her own strengths. For as long as she could remember, her father and her older brother had looked at her as if she were some plaster saint. She was always the good, compliant, pretty daughter and sister.

Part of that, of course, was her own fault. Her mother died when Rose was ten, and after that, she was in a constant state of fear that she would lose the rest of her family. That somehow, something would go wrong and she would be alone. She'd even convinced herself that if she wasn't perfect, they might not want her around at all.

So she had been better than perfect. She never made waves. Never questioned. Never argued. Never stood up for herself, not once. Even after college, she had maintained that air of perfection for her family and when her father had asked her to marry Henry Porter, she had agreed.

"Maybe Lucas King is just what you need," Dee was saying. "You've been celibate way too long. That creep of an ex-husband of yours really messed with your head and I'm thinking a little attention from the right person could just give you a whole new outlook."

Rose shook her head, took a sip of coffee and watched the neighbor's cat walk with balletic precision along the top of the block wall fence that separated the yards. She smiled to herself as the rotund calico paused long enough to bat one paw at a trembling leaf.

"What is whirling around in your devious mind?" Rose asked, though she knew she probably shouldn't.

"Seduction."

"What?"

"I'm just saying…if Lucas isn't a long-term guy, why can't he be a short-term one?"

"Because I work for him," Rose argued, shifting in her seat as a sudden surge of heat shot through her.

"Uh-huh, and one has nothing to do with the other," Dee insisted. "Live a little, sweetie. Have a fling. Enjoy. Don't you deserve some fun?"

Rose laughed. "Lucas? Fun? He's not an amusement park, Dee. He's…dangerous."

"Even better."

"You're hopeless."

"Thank you."

Rose heard the smile in her friend's voice and knew that Dee meant well, but… "I don't think so. I gave him the stay-away speech, remember?"

"Take it back."

"Hah! Just like that?"

"Why not? You said it was a great kiss."

"Practically a world record," Rose admitted, reliving that memory of his mouth locked with hers for what had to be the millionth time.

"One word from you, and I guarantee he'll forget all about your little hands-off speech."

"Then what?"

"Sweetie, if you have to ask that, it *has* been too long," Dee told her with a sigh. A second later, she said, "Oops, gotta run. My date's here."

"Right. Talk to you tomorrow."

"Okay, and Rose...live a little. Will you at least think about it?"

Once she hung up, Rose could acknowledge, at least to herself, that she would probably think of nothing else.

Five

"So we're agreed," Lucas said, glancing from Rafe to Sean. "We fire Warren."

"Hell yes," Sean muttered.

"Agreed," Rafe chimed in. "The man's used up his last chance with me. The mess he made out of the Johnson job is going to put us back at least two weeks. Not to mention we'll have to eat the cost of repairs to the water pipe and putting the yard back to rights."

"And there was water damage to the patio—redwood deck," Lucas reminded them.

"Perfect." Rafe sighed. "You know, we should fire him and send him over to work for Clancy's outfit. Serve 'em right."

Sean looked to Lucas, who shook his head firmly. He knew his youngest brother was about to tell Rafe all about Lucas's plan with Rose and, frankly, Lucas didn't want to hear it.

Naturally, that didn't stop Sean.

"Speaking of the Clancys," he said, shifting his gaze from Lucas to Rafe, "have you heard the latest? Big brother Lucas is taking cooking lessons from Rose Clancy, sainted sister of Devious Dave."

"Cooking lessons?" Rafe asked, confused. "Why the hell are you doing that? Hire somebody to cook for you if you can't figure it out yourself."

Lucas opened his mouth to speak, but Sean beat him to it. Really, now that he thought about it, he should have dropped Sean in the lake when they were kids.

"Oh, it's not just cooking Lucas is up to," Sean said quietly. "He's setting something up. Looking to use Rose as payback for what Dave did to us."

Rafe stared at him. "You're doing what?"

Lucas sighed and took a sip of his beer as Rafe went on a long-winded rant. He knew trying to interrupt would be pointless. Lucas didn't know how Katie, sweet woman that she was, could stand being married to the know-it-all. As the oldest of the three of them, Lucas was also the most patient of the three. He simply kept quiet and let Rafe go, knowing he'd eventually wind down and they could talk about this.

Once a week, the three King brothers who owned King Construction held a meeting to keep each other up-to-date on what was going on in the company. They rotated the meetings between each other's houses and this week, they were at Sean's place.

Great views, Lucas acknowledged, but then why wouldn't there be? Sean lived in a former water tower, which had been completely rehabbed and remodeled, of course. The water-tower home stood on a giant steel skeleton and the only way to the front door was a private elevator at street level. There was a wide, wraparound balcony surrounding the place, offering 360-degree views, and the living room where they sat boasted a wall of tinted windows that overlooked the ocean.

Out on the slate-gray waves beyond the glass, sailboats skimmed the surface and a few hardy surfers, outfitted in wetsuits, rode their boards into shore. From Lucas's perspective, the ocean scene looked peaceful and serene.

The direct opposite of the atmosphere here in Sean's coolly casual home. Everything had been going fine a few minutes ago. They'd wrapped up their business talk and after hearing yet another blissful take on the newlywed life from Rafe, Sean had mentioned what Lucas was up to with Rose.

That alone had been enough to throw a wrench into the conversation. Now, Rafe stared at Lucas from across the room and demanded again, "You're doing what with who?"

"Isn't that *whom?*" Sean said with a grin.

Rafe glared him into silence then turned his gaze back to Lucas. "Are you crazy?"

"Not the last time I checked, no." Lucas stood up, walked to the wet bar and poured a splash of single malt scotch into a crystal glass. He took a sip and turned to face his younger brother. "Dave Clancy cheated us. Used a spy in the company to steal contracts right out from under us. Why wouldn't I want to pay him back for that?"

"For God's sake, that was two years ago. Let it go already," Rafe said.

"Not a chance." Lucas bit the words out and felt the swell of indignation filling him.

Rafe was feeling magnanimous now, due to his happily married lifestyle. Two years ago, it had been a different story. Back then, all three of them had been furious and frustrated by the fact that they couldn't go after Dave legally because there was no evidence against him. Time passed and Rafe and Sean had both moved on, putting it behind them.

But for Lucas, the sting was still there. Maybe it was because *he* had been the one to introduce Dave to his brothers. *He* had been Dave's introduction to King Construction. Small wonder then that Lucas was taking this more personally than his brothers were.

"I tried to talk him out of it," Sean said. "But his head's as hard as Dad's."

"Nobody's head is that hard," Rafe said automatically, but kept his gaze fixed on Lucas. "If you're pissed at Dave, go after Dave. Using his sister is just sleazy."

"Exactly," Sean agreed.

A quick flicker of irritation spiked inside him because truthfully, it felt like that to Lucas sometimes, too. But the feeling wasn't strong enough to get him to back off.

"Rose is the way to make Dave pay. She's his baby sister. You remember how he was always bragging about her."

"Again," Rafe pointed out, "years ago."

"Family doesn't change."

"Amen to that," Sean muttered, then shrugged when Lucas stared at him. "Fine. Happy trails. Good luck on seducing then losing the lucky woman."

"Damn it, Sean…"

"Why be mad at him?" Rafe countered. "It's exactly what you're doing."

"Yeah?" Lucas met Rafe's stare and didn't give an inch. "And I seem to remember a guy whose plan was to topple the cookie queen into bed and then explain to her how all King men weren't jerks. Where were all your high standards then, Rafe?"

A flash of anger crossed Rafe's face at being reminded of how he'd tried to trick Katie when he first met her. But a second or two later, he said simply, "Yeah, you're right, and I almost lost her because of that stupid plan. You might want to think about that."

"Difference there is, I don't *want* to keep Rose," Lucas said. Not forever, anyway. But he wasn't in any hurry to send her on her way, either.

He scowled to himself at that thought. For a week now, Rose had been in his home every evening. They worked together in the kitchen. They talked, laughed and never once had either one of them brought up that staggering kiss they'd shared.

But it was there. Unsaid. Simmering in the air between them.

"Well, that makes it okay then," Rafe muttered.

"Yeah, were you planning on marrying Katie when you guys met? I don't think so." Lucas set his glass down and walked across the room to stand in front of Rafe. "I'm going to make sure Dave understands what stealing from a King means. And you're not going to talk me out of it."

"See?" Sean asked. "This is why I gave up trying to reason with either of you."

"Stay out of it, Sean," Lucas warned.

"Why the hell should I?" He stood up, too, and gave Lucas a hard stare. "You're not the only one Dave Clancy screwed. All three of us own the company. All three of us took a hit when he worked us over. But you *are* the only one acting like an ass about it."

Lucas bit down on his temper. Arguing with Rafe and Sean was pointless. They'd never understand why this was important to him. How could they? The three of them hadn't grown up together—none of Ben King's sons had—except for the summers all of them spent with Ben every year. And when those idyllic summers were over, Lucas went home to a woman who was constantly trusting the wrong men, only to have them break her heart.

Lucas had grown up with betrayal. He'd watched it happen to his mother over and over again and had finally realized that the only thing that really mattered in life was trust. Being able to trust those closest to you was priceless.

And no matter how angry he might be with his brothers, or them with him, he knew that they would be there for him, no matter what. For a man like Lucas, that was a gift beyond anything he could imagine.

The Kings stood together. No matter what.

It wasn't until two nights later that Rose appeared at Lucas's house. He saw her pull into the driveway and fought down a rush of expectation that he didn't want to either feel *or* acknowledge.

But it was damned hard to deny that he'd missed her. He hadn't seen her until now because she'd had standing cooking lessons to honor. She hadn't said with whom. It hadn't been with Kathy Robertson next door, though, and knowing that, Lucas had tortured himself, wondering if she was alone with some other guy. Cooking. Laughing. Talking.

Which was ridiculous, he knew. Why the hell should he care if she was at another man's house, spending time alone with him? She didn't belong to Lucas. They weren't a damn couple. She was, simply, a handy weapon he was preparing to wield.

And yet, he looked out the window and watched her lean into that silly van of hers with the skillet on the roof. His gaze locked on the curve of her behind and his groin tightened painfully. The ache of wanting her was stronger than ever.

Which should only help with the seduction plans, right?

When she straightened up and headed for the house, Lucas walked to the front door. He opened it and stood on the porch, waiting for her as she neared.

"Hi."

"Hi, yourself," he said, coming down the steps to take the heavy, cast-iron frying pan from her. "Why are you bringing your own pans? I've got plenty here."

"Ah, but you don't have a cast-iron skillet, and tonight, we need one."

They were stopped beneath the front porch light. Out on Pacific Coast Highway, cars streamed by, and on the sidewalk, a solitary woman walked a poodle so small it hardly qualified as a real dog.

But the rest of the world might as well have dropped away for all Lucas cared. His gaze was fixed only on Rose. Her eyes were bright, her lips curved into a smile and her long blond hair was loose around her shoulders. It was the first time he'd seen that thick mass free of the ponytail she usually wore and his hands itched to touch it. He wanted to wrap her hair around his hand and pull her in tight for a long, slow, deep kiss that would make the first one they'd shared look like a peck on the cheek.

He took a deep breath of the cold night air to try to dispel some of the heat charging through him. She got to him so fast and so completely, it kept catching him off guard, filling his mind with images that were designed to tempt and taunt him. Her scent drifted to him, and

Lucas's body hardened to the point of pain. In another minute, he'd be lucky to be able to walk to the kitchen.

If he wasn't careful, he might end up caught in his own trap. So to prove he was still in charge here, he pushed aside the urges rising within and forced himself to ask, "What are you planning for tonight, anyway?"

She looked a little startled at his gruff tone and he warned himself to dial it back. A second later, she edged past him into the house and headed for the kitchen without answering his question.

He knew what *his* plans would entail, but he didn't think she'd agree. At least, not yet. But soon, he promised himself as he turned and followed her into the house. His gaze locked on her retreating form, he repeated that vow silently.

Very soon.

"It's a surprise," she called back over her shoulder.

Lucas winced as he walked after her. He'd had enough surprises already, up to and including just how deeply he was being drawn into this little payback scheme. Many more surprises—without a little relief—and he'd be permanently in pain.

"Did you get my voice mail earlier?" Rose asked as he followed her down the long hallway, which was lined with framed family photos.

"If you mean did I take the steaks out of the freezer, yes," he answered. His gaze was locked on the fall of her hair, sliding down her back, swaying with her every step. On the curve of her hips, the lean length of her legs. He shook his head and swallowed a groan.

The flat heels of her shoes tapped against the wood floor and he liked the sound. Her steps were brisk, no-nonsense, and he had always liked a confident woman.

Funny, that wasn't how he remembered Rose, though.

When he'd first met her, she had seemed shy and a little standoffish. She'd hardly spoken to him the few times he'd seen her. But, he thought in retrospect, that had probably been due to Dave standing guard over her like a rabid pit bull.

He remembered being intrigued by her. He also remembered Dave shutting him down, fast. Back then, Rose's older brother had made it clear that she was off-limits. Now, Lucas had to wonder if she'd been off-limits only to *him*, since Dave was already planning on using Lucas to worm his way into a position of trust. Already planning on using the Kings and stealing from them.

And wondering that, Lucas had to also ask himself if Rose hadn't been in on it from the jump. Maybe, instead of being the carefully protected sister, she had been the bait in the trap. Beautiful. Seductive. Always kept out of reach, but dangled in front of a man until he stopped paying attention to whatever else was going on around him.

He watched her now through narrowed eyes, suspicion clawing at him. She moved around his kitchen, humming under her breath and even shuffling her feet into a little dance move to accompany whatever song was playing in her mind. She looked lovely. Innocent.

But how innocent could she really be? he wondered now. She was, after all, a Clancy.

Damn it, why had he never considered this before? Dave hadn't let Lucas get close to Rose, but he'd made damn sure that Lucas had had a good look at her. Can't catch anything if the victim never sees the bait.

Victim.

A rush of fury pushed through his veins. No. He wouldn't accept that. He wasn't a damn victim. He had been the target of an unscrupulous family. That didn't make him a victim. It made him...what, exactly? A fool for trusting? Well, he already knew that and accepted it.

The tide was about to turn, though. He'd get even with Dave for what he'd done to Lucas and the Kings. The upside was, now that he'd considered Rose might have been a part of the whole setup, he felt less...not guilt, precisely, but regret, about using her.

Lucas set her iron pan onto the stove with a clatter that got her attention. She whirled around and grinned at him. "You're going to love dinner tonight. And it's easy enough that you'll be able to make it again on your own anytime."

"Good to know." He tucked his hands into his jeans' pockets, leaned one hip against the edge of the black granite counter and watched her.

Frowning a little, she slipped out of the bright yellow windbreaker she wore over a cream-colored shirt and a pair of black jeans. "Is there something wrong?"

"No," he said with a shrug he hoped was convincing. "What could be wrong?"

"I don't know. You seem..." She paused, then shook her head. "Never mind."

Lucas told himself to lighten up. He didn't want to make her uneasy. Couldn't afford to scare her off before he had a chance to make her brother pay. So he smiled and offered, "Sorry. Bad day at work."

"What happened?"

"Why do you want to know?" he asked and wondered if she was reporting in to her brother on everything Lucas had to say. Then he scowled at himself and let that one go. There was such a thing as going overboard. Dave had already taken the Kings for all he was going to get. No doubt he'd forgotten all about them and had moved on to steal from someone else.

"Just curious, jeez," she said. "Thought you might want to talk about it, that's all. But no big deal if you don't."

"Sorry again," he said, shoving one hand through his hair. "I'm in a crappy mood and taking it out on you."

"It's okay, everybody needs to unload once in a while."

"Understanding of you," he muttered.

"Well, growing up in our house, believe me, I heard my father and Dave complaining all the time. I'm sort of used to it."

He didn't stiffen this time when she mentioned her brother, though damned if he didn't want to question her. Find out exactly what Dave had had to say about *him* two years ago. But he wouldn't. Not yet, anyway.

Instead, he gave her a brief description of the minor crises at King Construction. "One of the crews had to shut down. A retaining wall crumpled and a man was hurt."

Worry sparked in her eyes. "Is he going to be okay?"

"Yeah." Lucas shoved away from the counter, walked to the opposite side of the cooking island and looked at her. "Broke his leg in two places, though, so he'll be out for a while. Meanwhile, the crew was pulled out so a different one can go in tomorrow to reinforce the retaining wall. And there's a customer complaining about her new block wall fence. Seems when she told us to build it five-and-a-half-feet tall, what she really meant was six feet and we should have known."

She grimaced, then smiled in sympathy. "According to Dave, women customers are the worst."

"I don't know. I usually like working directly with

the woman of the house. Most times, she knows what she wants and she can make a decision quicker than her husband." He slapped both hands onto the cool granite. "Men tend to look at a situation from every possible angle. A woman will look, see what something needs and just do it."

She tipped her head to one side and studied him. "You were right before."

"About what?"

"When you said you were nothing like my brother," she told him.

In the overhead lights, her eyes blazed a clear, summer-sky blue. Her cheeks were still a little pink from the cold wind outside and when she licked her lips, a knot of something hot and needy settled inside Lucas.

It seemed, he thought, that every minute with Rose Clancy, he was fighting to maintain control. Something about this woman sneaked past every defense he had ever had in place, and despite suspecting that she might have had a hand in what Dave had done to the Kings two years ago—or maybe because of it—he wanted her. Bad.

When she reached behind her head to gather her hair into a ponytail, he stopped her.

"Leave it loose," he said quietly. "It's beautiful."

She blinked up at him, surprised by either his words or his tone…or both. Pleasure shone in her eyes and battled with the spark of confusion he could read in her expression.

"Thanks, but when I'm cooking it just gets in the way."

"Right." Lucas nodded and told himself to get a grip.

Yes, he was trying to seduce her, but he was also trying to stay clear of the web he already felt her spinning.

Women like her were dangerous, and Sean's warnings came flying back into his mind suddenly. Things like... *no way does this end well.*

Damned if he'd back away now, though. He took an emotional step back and changed the subject entirely. "So, what's the menu?"

She frowned, probably wondering why his tone had shifted so abruptly. But a moment later, she seemed to push aside any misgivings and said, "We're making steak quesadillas, Mexican rice and roasted asparagus."

"Well, you had me up until the asparagus."

She laughed. The sound rippled from her and seemed to drift through the kitchen. Lucas smiled and realized that he'd really missed her over the last couple of days. He hated like hell to admit that even to himself. But when she wasn't here, the big old house he loved felt... empty, in a way it never had before.

Easily explained, he assured himself silently while she gathered her hair into a ponytail, then moved around the kitchen with a familiar air.

Normally, he didn't bring women to his home. When he had a woman in his life, they either met at her place or wound up at a luxury hotel for the night. He didn't bring them here, because an invitation to his house sent out the wrong signals. The minute a woman started getting comfortable, she'd begin to think of what she had with Lucas as something more than temporary.

And it never was.

It wasn't just that, though. His gaze swept the kitchen quickly, taking it all in. This house was his sanctuary. His man cave, he guessed. And sharing it with a parade of women would only make it less than what it was to him.

"Serious thoughts?"

Caught, he glanced at her and shook his head.

"No," he lied. "Just watching the teacher. Making mental notes."

"Ah," she said with a quick smile. "Then step right up, student, and let's get to work."

Six

"That was *great*," Lucas said, lifting his glass of red wine for a long sip. "Seriously good."

"Thanks." Rose smiled to herself at the compliment. The dinner really had turned out well. "I hoped you would like them. You'll have to get a good cast-iron pan and then season it before you use it."

"Season it?"

"I'll show you how. But the cast iron makes all the difference when you're frying the quesadillas—makes them crisp and keeps the cheese-and-steak filling nice and hot. And when you make them for yourself, remember you can add diced green chilies if you want to spice them up a little."

"Nothing wrong with spicy," he said softly.

Rose got a chill just from the look in his eyes and the timbre of his voice. Any spicier right now, she thought, and she just might burst into flames.

He set his glass down, leaned his forearms on the table they shared beneath the big bay window and said, "You're a terrific cook, Rose. Why're you doing this when you could be running your own restaurant?"

"Oh..." She sat back, looked at him and sighed a little. "I admit, the thought of owning a restaurant and creating amazing dishes is wonderful. I actually wanted to go to the CIA—"

"And be a spy?"

She laughed. "Culinary Institute of America."

"Ah. Entirely different sort of classes then," he said, smiling.

"Completely."

"Why didn't you go?"

"Lots of reasons," she admitted, though she wouldn't go into specifics. What would be the point of telling him that at first her father and then Dave had submarined her plans. And then she had married Henry for all the wrong reasons, trapping herself in a marriage that was way less than happy. No, she didn't want to talk about any of that, so she said only, "Mainly, money. It's expensive, and I just can't do it right now."

"I don't get it," he said softly.

She read the confusion on his face and knew what he was thinking. Why would money be a problem for one of the Clancys? She had grown up wealthy and could be still, if she was willing to give up being her own boss and slide back under the protective and suffocating cloak her big brother wanted to throw over her.

"Doesn't matter," she said.

"Sure it does. You're a Clancy, Rose."

She didn't want to get into this. It was no one's business, after all. But sitting here in the dimly lit kitchen across the table from a gorgeous man looking at her with sincere interest in his gaze was hard to ignore.

"The truth is, I could go to the CIA if I were willing to move back into the family home and have Dave dictate my life for me."

"What?"

"Wow." She blew out a breath and laid one hand against the fluttering nerves in the pit of her stomach. "I can't believe I said that out loud."

"Well, you did," Lucas said, "and you can't leave it like that. Explain."

"Now that I've started," she agreed, "I really should explain. Look, I know you and Dave don't speak anymore…"

His features iced over in a blink.

"And, I can tell by your expression you don't want to talk about that. But let me just say, I love my brother. He's always been good to me. He's just a little…"

"Overbearing?" Lucas supplied.

"Overprotective," she corrected. "And since Dad died, Dave's gotten worse."

"I was sorry to hear about your dad," Lucas murmured.

She looked up into his eyes and did read genuine regret there, and she was pleased. Whatever had gone wrong between Lucas and her brother, at least he wasn't taking it out on *her*. Staring at him across the table now, she felt at ease with him as she didn't with many people—men, especially.

Usually the men she met were after something. They wanted to use her to get to her brother. Coming from money wasn't always the happy thing that most people imagined it would be. For one thing, you never knew if someone liked you for yourself or for your bank account.

Which, she admitted with a rueful inner smile, wasn't a problem for her these days. Not since she'd cut herself off from the family coffers to go her own way.

"Anyway," she said, inhaling sharply to bring her mind back into line. "The bottom line is, after my divorce I told Dave what I wanted to do and he actually tried to tell me no. That I should do volunteer work— not that there's anything wrong with that at all," she added quickly. "But I wanted more. I wanted to build my own business. Be my own boss. And Dave thought it was too risky to invest in."

He snorted his disgust.

She appreciated the gesture even though she had the strangest urge to defend her brother. Shaking her head free of that notion, she said simply, "So I took the small trust fund my grandmother left me, opened my own business and am now alternately sinking and swimming all by myself."

"Good for you," he said, leaning back in his chair. "I can admire someone who knows what they want and goes after it."

"Thanks. Wish Dave felt the same," she admitted and felt a ball of tension in her stomach disappear.

"Yeah, well, Dave's a special case, isn't he?" Lucas muttered.

Studying him, she said softly, "I told you my deep dark secrets…why don't you tell me what happened between you and my brother to break up your friendship?"

"No."

"Just 'no'?"

"Get Dave to tell you," he said.

"Yeah, he won't talk about you, either," Rose told

him. She tossed her ponytail back over her shoulder and said, "Secrets usually come out though. Eventually."

"Not if you're careful," Lucas said, meeting her gaze until she was forced to look away from the heat she could see in those deep blue eyes.

"And you are?" she asked. "A careful man, I mean?"

"Always," he said, leaning toward her. "I'm a King. We might make mistakes, but we never make the same ones twice."

She looked up at him and tried to read what she saw in his eyes, but there was an emotional barrier there that she couldn't see past. There was more to his statement than she knew, Rose told herself. But getting any more out of him wouldn't be easy.

There was a warm, intimate feeling between them right now, she thought. Maybe it was the soft lighting, or the darkness beyond the windows. But it felt as though they were the only two people in the world. And that was a dangerous feeling, she realized.

Lucas King was temptation personified. Even his usually gruff manner wasn't enough to dispel the fantasies that seemed to arise with more and more frequency lately. Then Rose thought about everything Dee had said about maybe just "living a little." Why not enjoy Lucas in the short term?

Her stomach spun as she actually entertained the idea of seducing Lucas King. Could she do it? Hah! Of course she could do it. She'd seen the way he looked at her. She felt the heat pouring from his body into hers every time they so much as brushed against each other.

Oh, more and more dangerous, she thought, and said abruptly, "You know, I really should straighten up."

She bolted from her chair and with her back to Lucas, she grimaced tightly at her own cowardice. She had thought about this man for years and now that she had the opportunity to do something about it, what did she do? *The dishes.*

Flipping the water faucet on, she was grateful for the rush of water into the sink. At least the soft roar filled the silence. Then she heard Lucas walking up behind her and she braced herself. *Be strong,* she told herself silently.

"Don't," he said.

Startled, Rose wondered if she'd actually spoken aloud, but in the next moment, Lucas reached past her, turned the water off and said, "Don't hide from what's happening."

"Lucas..."

"You don't want to do the dishes, Rose," he murmured into the strained quiet. Then he laid his hands on her shoulders and turned her around to face him.

Stomach swirling, mouth dry, she lifted her gaze to his and inhaled sharply. Desire played out in those cool blue depths and he was making no effort to disguise his need for her.

"I've wanted to do this since that first night we kissed," he whispered and bent down slowly, lowering his mouth to hers.

Rose felt her heartbeat jump into overdrive as Lucas got even closer. Her hands were braced on the edge of the counter behind her, her chest heaving with each shallow breath she took. Heat zoomed through her until she felt like a sudden fever had slapped her.

His mouth was just a breath away from hers when her mind started racing.

Did she dare risk a very good-paying job for the momentary satisfaction of having the night she'd always dreamed of with Lucas King?

Did she dare *not* do it when she had the chance?

Did she want to live to be a hundred and go to bed every night, filled with regrets, asking herself. *Why didn't you sleep with that man?*

No. She really didn't.

"Rose?"

He had stopped, his lips a fraction of an inch from hers. Waiting. Waiting for her to be the one to decide. For her to put a stop to this or welcome him with open arms.

He lifted one hand, smoothed his fingertips across her cheek and instantly, wild heat skittered through her body. Want and need clawed at her.

Lucas King's touch was magnetic. Electric.

And just like that, her decision was made.

"No more hiding," she whispered and leaned into him, offering her mouth up to him. And as his lips closed over hers, she sighed.

She was ready for the electricity.

She was more than ready for Lucas King.

He cupped her face in his palms and kissed her so thoroughly, so completely, Rose was lost in the sensations whipping through her. If she hadn't already made up her mind to do this, the kiss would have convinced her. This kiss shook her completely, even more than the one they had shared only the week before, and, until that moment, she wouldn't have thought that possible.

A desperate sort of longing filled her. This was what she'd been looking for most of her life. This…magic that sent waves of pleasure crashing through her. Rose leaned into him, wanting more, wanting it all. Heat pooled in her center along with a throbbing ache that pulsed in time with the ragged beat of her heart.

Rose's skin hummed with anticipation as her tongue tangled with his. Lucas growled low in his throat and that rumble of sound awakened something vital inside her. His response to her was every bit as intense as her own. Knowing that, *feeling* that, gave her a heady sense of feminine power like she had never experienced before.

Always, she had been the good girl. The one that men treated like either a friend or a nun. Even her ex-husband had never really wanted her. But tonight, Lucas was changing all of that. Until him, no one had ever made her feel so sensual. So *desired*. Her dreams of Lucas from so long ago were now splintered beneath the reality. His hands slid down her neck, over her shoulders and around to stroke frantically up and down her back as if he couldn't touch her enough. She shivered with pleasure, yet wanted more. She wanted to feel his hands on her skin. Feel the hard brush of his palms against her naked flesh.

Crazy, her mind whispered.

Quiet, her body answered.

He tore his mouth from hers and lowered his head to nibble at the line of her throat. Rose arched her neck to one side to give him easier access. A second later, he groaned, lifted the hem of her shirt and pulled it up and over her head. She raised her arms to help, needing to feel his body against hers.

She didn't care that this was all happening too fast for her to think her way out of it. She didn't *want* to stop and be rational. For once in her life, Rose simply wanted to surrender to the thing she craved.

"I need you, Rose," he whispered, shifting his

hands to cup her lace-covered breasts. His thumbs and forefingers toyed with her sensitive nipples and even through her bra, the sensations were almost too much to bear.

He couldn't have said anything more perfect, she thought. Rose opened her eyes, looked up into his and said, "Yes, Lucas. I need you, too. Now."

"Good. That's good." He kissed her, hard, fast. A half smile curved his mouth briefly before intensity filled his gaze and he said, "Be sure, Rose. Once we start, neither one of us is going to want to stop."

"Nobody's stopping," she promised him, reaching out to stroke her hands over his chest.

He sucked in a gulp of air, gritted his teeth and said, "Thank God."

Reaching behind her, he unhooked her bra in a smooth, practiced move and then pushed it down and off her arms. He took a long look at her then and Rose felt his gaze as surely as she would have a touch.

"You, too," she said, tugging at his T-shirt. He nodded, yanked it off and tossed it to the floor behind him.

Rose sighed and enjoyed the view briefly before Lucas grabbed her and pulled her in close.

Skin to skin.

The friction was almost unbearable. He dropped his head to her shoulder and then pulled her head to one side so he could kiss and lick and nibble at her throat again. Rose couldn't breathe. With his hands on her, his mouth moving over her, she couldn't find any air and, oddly enough, she didn't care. Nothing mattered beyond the next kiss. The next caress. Time slipped away. The world disappeared.

All that existed was this moment.

This man.

Her mind went blessedly blank under the furious assault of too many sensations to keep track of.

"You feel so good," he murmured, splaying his hands against her back before letting them drop to the curve of her behind. He pulled her in close, aligning her body along his until she felt his hard length pressing against her abdomen and knew he was swamped by the same desperate need as she was.

"Not in the damn kitchen," he muttered.

Rose didn't care where they were. They could have been outside under the streetlights with neighbors sitting on their front porches watching and she wouldn't have cared. She just wanted his hands on her. His body moving inside hers. "Doesn't matter."

"Yeah, it does. Upstairs," he ordered, grabbing one of her hands and pulling her behind him as he headed for the hallway and the stairs.

Half-dressed, wild with desire, Rose kept up with him, but just barely. His long legs covered a lot more territory than she could. She stumbled, and wasn't surprised since her knees felt wobbly enough to collapse on her at any moment.

"Slow down," she finally said.

"Not an option," he groaned and whirled around to face her. "I already feel like I've been waiting years for this. No slowing down," he told her, jaw clenched. "No rethinking. No backing out."

His gaze was blue fire. Burning, glittering with more heat than she had ever seen before and everything in her roared to the surface to meet it.

She shook her head and said only, "You're walking too fast, I can't keep up."

He flashed her a quick smile that was born and gone again in an instant. "Why didn't you say so?"

He picked her up and swung her into the cradle of his arms, and Rose was absolutely romanced down to her soul.

He took the stairs two at a time, reaching the landing in a few long strides. Held close to his chest, Rose glanced briefly at his face as he stalked down the hall to the closed door at the far end. Even in her sexual haze, she noted her surroundings as they passed. Cream-colored walls, cherry-wood crown molding and a gleaming wood floor, covered by a deep red floor runner that muffled Lucas's steps as he relentlessly headed for their destination.

"Almost there," he murmured and Rose nodded, lifting one hand to smooth it over the sculpted muscles of his chest.

This wasn't a man born to wear a suit, she thought idly, while her fingertips moved across his skin, smoothing through the thatch of dark hair. His skin was bronzed as if he'd spent years in the sun and she could only imagine that the hard, chiseled planes of his chest had been born working on construction sites.

Her thumb moved over one flat nipple and he hissed in a breath as he kicked the bedroom door open, sending it slamming into the wall behind.

"Do that again and this is going to be over a lot sooner than either one of us wants it to be," he warned as his arms tightened around her like bands of iron.

That promise sent even more heat to her center, and she squirmed in his arms at the sudden discomfort of her jeans. She wanted. Needed. She took a breath and looked around. The huge room was darkened but for the moonlight pouring through the wide windows onto a gigantic bed. She didn't notice anything else.

Her gaze shifted to him and locked there as he stopped at the side of the bed, reached down and threw back the black duvet to reveal crisp white sheets. Mounds of pillows banked against the headboard and when he dropped her onto the mattress, Rose bounced a couple of times, still never taking her eyes from his.

Her entire body was sizzling. She swallowed hard at the look in his eyes. She felt like a banquet laid out before a starving man and heaven help her, she couldn't wait for him to take his first bite.

Desire pumped through her, making every nerve ending feel as though it was on fire.

"I've been thinking about this—you, here in my bed—for almost two weeks," he admitted, bending over her as she unsnapped her jeans then pulled the zipper down. He pulled the jeans and her panties off, pausing only long enough to tear her shoes off and toss them aside as well.

"I have, too," she admitted, though if she were going to be completely honest with him—which she wasn't— she'd have to say she had been thinking about this moment for three *years*. Since the moment her brother had introduced them and then metaphorically hung a No Trespassing sign over her head.

"Wait's over," he grumbled and peeled out of his own clothes in a heartbeat of time.

"Thank goodness," she whispered. Her gaze moved over him in a blink and everything hot and needy inside her stirred into frantic life. His body was amazing. She couldn't wait to feel it moving within her.

She lifted her arms in welcome and he bent over her, joining her on the wide bed, sliding his hands up and down her body, exploring every curve, learning every line. His breath came hot and fast against her neck, her breasts, as he took first one nipple then the other into his mouth, lavishing each of them with attention. His teeth scraped across the sensitive tips, and his tongue worked her until she was whimpering beneath the onslaught of feelings. He suckled her and it felt as though he were drawing her essence into his mouth. She clung to him, holding his head in place while her body arched and shifted on the cool sheets, looking blindly for release.

He fed off her response, ramping up his touch, his kisses. As if he felt everything she was experiencing, Lucas seemed to know just how to touch her. How to stroke and caress until she was babbling helplessly.

She writhed beneath him, hips rocking, back arching, moving into him, wanting, needing. Her mind shut down to everything but the incredible sensations he brought her. His hands seemed to be everywhere at once. Her breasts, her nipples, her abdomen, her… "Lucas—"

His big hand cupped her core and she gasped his name again, louder this time. Finally, her body seemed to shout. At last. What she needed. His thumb rubbed that small, sensitive bud at her center as he dipped first one finger and then two into her heated depths.

"Lucas, please," she whispered brokenly, hips moving into his hand, her head turning from side to side on the bed as she fought for breath, fought for completion.

Spirals of tension coiled inside her with every stroke of his fingers. He dipped his head to claim one of her nipples again and as he suckled her, he rubbed even harder at her center and the two sensations combined made Rose absolutely mindless with craving.

She moaned his name and fisted her hands in the sheet beneath her, trying to keep her grip on her unsteady world. Feet planted on the mattress, she rocked her hips ceaselessly, hungering for a release that remained tantalizingly out of reach. She worked for it, practically wept for it as each breath she drew grew shallower, more desperate.

He lifted his head, looked at her and in his eyes she saw the same frantic need she was feeling. "Fast and hard, that's how I want you, Rose."

"Yes. Be inside me. Now. Please," she whispered, twisting beneath him, parting her thighs even wider, her body issuing the invitation she couldn't find the breath to speak.

He reached over to the bedside table, yanked open the drawer and pulled out a condom. He tore the wrapping open, grabbed the latex and sheathed himself in one quick move.

"A careful man," she whispered, echoing the words he'd once said to her.

"You make me crazy, Rose," he muttered darkly, moving to cover her body with his.

She smiled, stupidly pleased by that remark. "I do?"

"Yeah. Hell, I almost forgot to grab a condom," he admitted, taking her mouth in a long kiss as his body slid into her heat.

"Oh, my…" She arched into him, lifting her hands to his shoulders, clinging to him as if she needed his strength to hold her onto the planet.

"Rose…" He groaned and held perfectly still for one heart-stopping moment. "Can't wait. Have to have you," he said on a sigh and, almost instantly, set a fast, hard rhythm that had Rose's heart racing. Again and again, he entered and withdrew. Their bodies moved together in the moonlight, each of them reaching for completion. Each of them clinging to the other.

And as the last, taut coil of tension inside her suddenly exploded, Rose called out his name and looked up into his eyes as the rest of the world fell away. A crashing wave of staggering pleasure washed through her, leaving her shaken and vulnerable.

She was still holding him, still meeting that passion-fueled gaze, when his body erupted into hers and, cradling him, Rose rode the wave of his release as fully as she had her own.

Seven

Lucas felt as though he'd just run a marathon.

His body still locked inside hers, his climax still rippling through his body, he hardened for her again. Rocking into her, he heard her sigh and felt her hook her legs at the small of his back.

"Mmm…" Her satisfied sigh rattled him, and at the same time fed the burgeoning hunger that was refueling itself inside him.

He groaned again and knew they weren't finished. A part of him wondered if they would *ever* be finished.

She flattened her palms against his chest and stroked his skin—her touch was like silk. He looked into her eyes and saw the passion-glazed stare of a woman completely undone and should have felt a jolt of satisfaction for a plan that was coming together all too well.

Instead, all he felt was more want. More need.

Her blue eyes were shining with every ounce of passion that was flaring inside him. She wanted him again every bit as much as he wanted her. The smoldering fire between them leaped into life like an inferno. Her short, neat fingernails scratched at his skin and every single touch was like the lick of flames. She thumbed one of his nipples and he felt the jolt of renewed passion zip through him like a lightning strike.

Heartbeat pounding, he took her mouth again. Their tongues tangled together, breath sliding from one to the other of them. Each of them fought their own need and offered it up to the other. Each of them hungered and Lucas did the only thing he could. He moved inside her again and heard her groan of satisfaction as his reward.

This wasn't seduction anymore.

This was *need*. Crashing, burning desperation—and it wouldn't be denied.

Easing up a bit, he unhooked her legs from his waist and draped them over his shoulders. She licked her lips and rocked her body on his, sliding him in even deeper than he had been.

Lucas hissed in a breath and fought for the legendary calm that seemed to have completely deserted him. When it came to this woman, he had no control. How could he have not noticed that before?

He was always in control. Always cool and composed. Distanced even, from the very women he slept with. There were barriers erected between him and the rest of the world.

But tonight was different.

She was different.

There was nothing he wouldn't do to have Rose, Lucas thought. For the first time *ever,* his mind was taking a backseat to his body's demands and he didn't care. Didn't want to think and could only be grateful for the complete shutdown of his coolly rational brain.

"Lucas…"

Her whispered plea slammed into him. He reached for their joining and stroked his thumb over the one nub of flesh he knew would make her the most crazed. She didn't disappoint him. Instantly, she rocked on him, swiveling her hips as best she could to take him deeper, higher.

And still it wasn't enough.

Shifting position, Lucas pulled free of her, drawing moans from both of them. Then he eased her legs off his shoulders, turned her over onto her stomach and lifted her hips.

Moving to accommodate what he was doing, Rose went up on all fours and in an instant, Lucas entered her body again, seating himself as deeply as he could. His hands on her behind, he squeezed and stroked while she moved into him, gasping for every breath.

He slid one hand down and around to cup one of her breasts, tugging at her nipple as he continued to move inside her. Faster, harder, deeper, he pushed them both beyond the edge of reason and into a world where the only hope either of them had was another crushing release.

Moonlight caressed her skin and silvered her hair. The cool sheets beneath them and the chill of the air in the room added even more sensation to what passed between them. And when he felt her climax stir, Lucas let himself go. This time when they made that leap, they made it together.

A few minutes later, Lucas was lying against the bank of pillows with Rose still spooned in front of him. He hadn't been able to separate himself from her yet. The heat of her drew him in and it was something he was in no hurry to give up. Breath churning from his lungs, he fought to get his brain back. He'd never experienced anything like this before. Rose was the first woman in his life that had emptied his mind and fired his body so that nothing else had mattered.

He could hardly believe what had happened. He hadn't been able to dredge up coherent thought beyond admitting to himself that she was so much more than he had originally thought. His natural restraint had dissolved. His rational self had taken a vacation, leaving his body in charge—and he hardly knew what to think about that. Hell he'd never lost himself in a woman like that before. Sighing, he kissed her shoulder and reluctantly parted them. And—

A sudden, staggering realization punched him hard. How could he have not noticed? Been so careless?

Looking down at the woman cuddled into him he said, "Rose, tell me you're on the pill."

"What?" She sighed, rolled over and nestled her head more comfortably on his chest then licked her lips.

That brief sweep of her tongue sent another jolt of desire through him and he had to fight to ignore it.

"The pill, Rose," he repeated as she shifted lazily to turn her gaze up to his.

Her hair was a cloud of silvery blond, framing her face and lying across her pale, beautiful skin, making her look like some pagan goddess. And, despite the raging unease inside him, his body instantly went like stone again. If he wasn't careful, he was going to be repeating his stupendous lack of control.

"What did you say?" She stroked her palm up his

chest and around to his back and the brush of her fingertips against his skin felt like match flames.

He hissed in a breath, caught her wandering hand in his and growled, "Rose, the damn condom *broke*. Tell me you're on the pill."

That got her attention. She went absolutely still and her eyes widened. His stomach sank. He saw the flash of shock that became worry in her eyes, and he knew they were in trouble.

"Oh, God…" She pulled her hand free of his grip and covered her mouth with it.

Lucas sighed and briefly dropped one arm across his eyes as if he could shut out the whole image of what had just happened. He couldn't believe this.

"How did it…never mind."

"I don't know how the hell it broke, either," he muttered. "It's never happened to me before." He got out of bed, stalked to the bathroom to take care of the mess, then headed back to the bedroom. Sitting on the bed, he pulled her into his side and looked down at her. "Look, it's too late for this conversation, but you should know I'm healthy."

"Me, too," she assured him, though he hadn't for a second considered she might not be.

Not the sweet and pure Rose.

Irritation warred with the dregs of the passion he was still feeling. Even now, when he was reeling with the possibilities facing him, Lucas could admit to himself that his desire for her hadn't been quenched. Not even close. Which said exactly what about him?

She pushed her hair out of her face and reached for the edge of the duvet, dragging it up over her breasts as if somehow by draping herself in armor she could undo what they had already done.

"Is there a chance?" He actually winced at what had to be the dumbest question he'd ever uttered. Of course there was a chance she would get pregnant. He'd been stupid. Thoughtless. Allowed himself to be carried away by his body's demands at the expense of his damn brain.

"Forget it," he said quickly. "Stupid question. I know there's a chance."

"It's the wrong time of the month," she told him, "but that's no guarantee...." A moment later, she groaned and added, "I can't believe it broke."

His teeth clenched hard enough to snap his jaw, but he still managed to say, "My fault."

"Oh, please."

Not the reaction he'd expected. When he looked at her closely he was even more surprised by the irritated expression she was aiming at him.

"We're both grown-ups, Lucas. We were both here. We both wanted this and neither one of us handmade a faulty condom, so please don't treat me like a child and take all the blame for this."

"That's not how I meant it," he muttered. Women were damned confusing at times, he told himself. You don't take responsibility, they're pissed. You *do* take it and they're pissed anyway.

"Well, it's what you said," she told him, swinging her hair back from her face. "My God, you don't even see how insulting that is, do you? What? Am I some airhead who doesn't know how babies are made? Is that it?"

"No, damn it, what are you so mad about?"

"Oh, this is just typical," she muttered darkly, her hands fisting on the duvet until her knuckles went white. "I'm so tired of everyone around me acting as though I'm a porcelain doll or something. No mind of my own."

She scooted off the bed, still clutching the duvet tightly to her. "My father, my ex, Dave and now *you*."

He jumped off the bed, too, and stood there naked, watching her stomp barefooted around the edge of the mattress. "Don't lump me in with them."

"If it walks like a duck…"

"Great. Perfect." He threw his hands up and shook his head. Weirdest damn after-sex conversation he'd ever had. "You're an intelligent woman in charge of herself who might be pregnant because of a faulty condom. Happy?"

"Delirious," she snapped. "You just don't get it. I spent most of my life taking orders from the men in my life, who insisted they knew better than I did. I didn't argue, either, which is totally my fault," she added in a disgusted undertone. "I even married a man my father picked out because I didn't want to disappoint him."

Lucas shoved one hand through his hair. "Always wondered why you married that jerk."

"Now you know. Spineless Rose. That was me," she said with a shudder. "I look back and even I don't believe what a doormat I was." Flashing him a look that should have set him on fire, she added, "But you know what? Being married to Henry, living through the humiliation of him constantly cheating on me, was a valuable lesson."

"In what? Torture? Self-sacrifice?" He snorted a laugh. "Figures Saint Rose would find the silver lining in the middle of the storm."

She inhaled sharply and her expression was horrified. "*Saint Rose?* That's what you think of me?"

"That's what everyone thinks of you. The good. The perfect. The always proper and demure Rose Clancy," he said, despite the voice in his head warning him to step carefully.

She kicked the duvet away from her feet and, still clutching the top of it to her breasts, marched over to him, fury stamped on her features. When she was close enough, she poked him in the chest with her index finger.

Didn't look demure now, Lucas thought warily. Her eyes were flashing and her mouth was flattened into a thin, straight line that told him he was lucky she wasn't armed.

"I'm no saint," she snapped, defining each word with a sharp stab of her finger.

"I'm getting that."

"And I'm not the same Rose you used to know. I'm done taking orders from men—*any* man." She gave him a shove that didn't budge him an inch. "I'll make my own decisions, and I'll worry about my own mistakes, and I don't need you telling me what to do."

He crossed his arms over his chest and glared down at her. "Fine. Make your decision. Start with what do we do now."

"What do you mean?" she asked with a choked-off laugh that sounded just this side of hysterical. "There's nothing to do. It's done. A little late to be locking the old barn door, don't you think?"

"Yeah." He scrubbed one hand across the back of his neck and nodded to himself. "We'll just see what happens and if you are pregnant, then we'll get married and…"

"*Married?* What? You'll throw yourself on a funeral pyre? Gee, thanks. I feel so much better now." Shaking her head, she added in an undertone, "Ten seconds and he's back to treating me like an idiot again."

"How am I treating you like an idiot?"

"Hah! Just look at you. Acting like—" her voice dropped to a poor imitation of a man's "—poor, helpless Rose. I mistreated her badly. Better find a way to make it up to her." She slumped over dramatically. "I know! I'll just fall on my sword. That should take care of things."

"What the hell—"

She straightened up and flashed him another look that promised all sorts of retribution. "I don't need you sacrificing yourself for me, okay? It was sex. Great, earth-shaking and as it turns out, *unprotected* sex. I can deal. What I am not going to do is marry another man for all the wrong reasons. So come on out of the nineteenth century, Lucas."

He'd listened to her, dumbfounded, while she went on her rant. Well, now it was his turn. "Maybe this isn't about what *you* can deal with, Rose. Ever consider that?"

Turning his back on her, he scanned the floor for his jeans and grabbed them up. Shifting back to face her again as he pulled them on, he kept talking, irritated not just with himself, but also with the woman who only moments ago had had his engines roaring.

"Do you know who my father is?"

"What?" She scowled at him. "What does that have to do with—"

"Ben King, that's who," Lucas told her, shoving both hands through his hair with nearly enough heat to pull out every strand. "Ben King is to illegitimate sons what Johnny Appleseed was to trees. Do you get it now? Do you see why I'm taking responsibility for this?"

"No! What does your father have to do with anything that happens between us?"

He stomped to her side, noting that she held the duvet

higher and closer to her chest. The image of her as a pagan goddess slammed into him again. Moonlight sifting over her, outlining her in silver until she didn't even look real. She looked, actually, like every man's dream woman. Rumpled and sexy and ready to be tossed onto the nearest bed.

Which is just what he wanted to do.

Instead, he grabbed her bare shoulders and felt the heat of her blast into his hands. "My father spread his sperm in such a wide swath, we haven't even *met* all of our brothers yet," he told her flatly. "I promised myself years ago that I would never do that. I would never create a child that wasn't wanted. Planned for. *Loved*."

Her features clouded up briefly, but her eyes had lost their fire when she said, "Okay, I can understand that, but Lucas, you did the right thing. You were thinking. I sure as heck wasn't. Protection never occurred to me, I'm ashamed to say. You thought of it."

"For all the good it did us. Doesn't change anything," he muttered and released her because if he held on to her any longer, he might not be able to let go at all. "If we made a child tonight, we're getting married. I'm not having any kid of mine grow up like I did. With a part-time father and a mother who spent all of her time trying to find a man to stay with her."

He'd never said that out loud before. Never let anyone catch a glimpse of the kind of childhood he'd had. Lucas had loved his parents, but he wasn't born blind. His mom was a nice woman who hadn't been strong enough to be a single mother. She had spent every waking moment looking for the love that Ben King hadn't been able to give her.

He wouldn't sentence any child of his to the kind of half life Lucas had known as a kid.

As if she sensed just how ragged he was feeling, Rose let her anger fade away. Her voice softened, too, as she said, "We're not going to settle anything tonight, Lucas. And we're probably going to war over nothing. I think I should just go."

Her skin looked milky against the dark fabric she held so tightly and her hair was as pale as the moonlight. Her eyes were shadowed, though, and he hated to see it.

His seduction plan had worked too well. Not only had he gotten Rose into his bed, but he'd also been seduced. Losing himself in the feel of her. The taste of her. Even now, knowing what they might be facing, his body ached for her again. His brain was racing, but his body only *needed*.

Nothing about Rose Clancy was turning out to be easy.

"Maybe we should talk this out more."

"I think we've already said plenty." She glanced around the room looking for her clothes. She grabbed her panties and jeans and tugged them on, then seemed to realize that they had left their shirts downstairs.

"Oh, for heaven's sake," she muttered, crossing her arms over her breasts. "I don't even have my shirt with me. What was I thinking?"

The problem was, Lucas thought, that neither of them had been thinking at all. This whole seduction thing had gotten way out of hand. He'd thought he was in charge. Totally on top of the situation. What a joke. Now he was caught in a web of his own making and he didn't have a clue as to whether there was a way out or not—or hell, whether or not he even *wanted* a way out.

Which was so far out of orbit for him, he dismissed the thought the minute it rose up in his mind. This was not about forever. Hell, this wasn't even temporary. This was just supposed to be a one-night seduction and then revenge. Plain and simple.

Only problem was, *simple* was off the table.

"You know what?" Rose was saying, shaking her head as if she couldn't believe she was standing there half-dressed. "I just have to go. Now."

Only minutes ago this woman had practically set his bed on fire. Now they were awkward with each other, neither of them sure of their next move. And for Lucas at least, that was a first.

"No point in hiding your breasts from me now, is there?" he asked, taking her elbow to escort her downstairs.

"In bed, it's different. Just standing here..." She closed her eyes and huffed out a breath that could have been anger but was probably embarrassment.

He snatched up a T-shirt off a chair in his room and handed it to her. "Here."

"Thanks," she muttered, turning her back on him to pull his shirt over her head. The hem of the dark green shirt fell to the middle of her thighs and made her look smaller, more vulnerable somehow—and he didn't think she'd like knowing that.

When she looked at him again, she refused to meet his gaze. Everything had changed now. They'd let each other in and exposed too many secrets and now they were both busily rebuilding personal barriers. Lucas steered her out of his room and down the hall, sensing the emotional distance between them as they walked in strained silence.

And all he could think was that Sean had been right. Revenge really did have a way of turning around to bite you in the ass.

* * *

Staring at the computer screen doing the books for her business wasn't taking Rose's mind off of Lucas King. She rubbed her gritty eyes, shook her head and tried to focus again, but even she could see it was useless.

Everything on the screen might as well have been in Greek. Numbers seemed to run together. Red and black. Clients and suppliers. Appointments and schedules. All of it was blurred into a distorted mess that seemed to taunt her feelings of ineptitude. That's what she got for trying to work when she was so tired she could hardly see straight.

"But to be fair," she said aloud in the stillness, "I suck at this end of the business even on a good day."

Frowning, she kicked back in her chair, lifting her sneaker-clad feet to the corner of her desk. Her small home office was brutally organized. Not a paper out of place. There were file cabinets, a three-in-one copier/printer/fax machine and a top-of-the-line computer on a simple wood desk. She glanced at the framed poster of Ireland hanging on the wall and briefly wished she were there on that rocky coast, with the wind in her hair.

But that thought only lasted a moment as she sighed and glanced around the room. She had been so determined, when she started Home Cooking Taught at Home, to be the quintessential businesswoman. And for a while, she had made a good job of it. Until last night. Rose was pretty sure *quintessential* didn't mean sleeping with your clients—or rather *not* sleeping, but having amazing, soul-shaking, body-burning sex.

Her feet dropped to the floor as her stomach pitched. "Oh, God." She lowered her head to the desk until her forehead hit with a *thunk*. Rose sat up abruptly, reaching to rub her forehead.

She could be pregnant.

"No, don't think that, and for heaven's sake, don't say it out *loud*," she whispered, shaking her head. All she needed was to throw that challenge out to the universe.

Pregnancy was *not* in her business plan. Or in her life plan for that matter. Sure, someday, she'd love to have children. Had always wanted them, in fact…but not yet. She knew there were women out there who managed to be single moms and work and have a life and pull it off beautifully.

But that's not what she wanted.

Even with her miserable marriage in her background, Rose still wanted the fairy tale.

"Of course, they were called *Grimm* fairy tales for a reason," she told herself with a sigh. Oh, yeah, she was in great shape. Her mind wandering down long, twisting paths that went exactly nowhere and made her feel absolutely no better.

Trying to work was pointless, she finally admitted. No way was she going to be able to concentrate. Her gaze shifted to the noticeably silent phone on the corner of her desk. She had half expected Lucas to call and didn't know what she would say to him if he did. But the fact that he hadn't was beginning to really tick her off.

What had happened at his house after she left last night? Did he crawl right back into bed and sleep like a baby? No worries? No thoughts about her or them or what might be happening inside her body right at this minute? Was he really that cold? Was he so unemotional he couldn't even be bothered to call and say, "Hey, you okay? How's the baby?"

"He's right. Women aren't logical," she mused, pushing out of her chair to walk into the kitchen. "But how are we supposed to be logical when dealing with *men?*"

Her own kitchen was much smaller than the one at Lucas's house. But it was cozy and familiar and on this foggy, gray morning, it felt like sunshine with its white and yellow walls.

She filled the teakettle at the sink, set it on the stove and turned the fire on underneath it. While she waited for the water to boil, Rose leaned back against the counter, folded her arms over her chest and wondered what she was supposed to do now.

"Excellent timing," she murmured. "Why didn't you do some thinking last night when it might have helped? Because," she added ruefully, "you were too busy *feeling* to want to do anything rational."

Oh, terrific. Not only was her world sort of crumbling down around her, but now she was also talking to herself. That couldn't be a good sign.

Plus she was exhausted. She had been up all night. Every time she had closed her eyes, she saw Lucas. Heard his voice. Felt his hands on her body.

If she had managed to fall asleep, no doubt her dreams would have been in 3D with surround sound. So instead, she'd spent the last several hours cleaning her house until it was shining and then watching infomercials on television. Now her eyes felt like two marbles left out in the sun too long and fatigue dragged at every muscle.

Steam pushed out the spout of the teakettle, making an ear-piercing noise that shattered her thoughts and got her moving again. She took the kettle off the flame, poured the boiling water into her waiting teacup and idly stood there while the lone decaf tea bag brewed. She'd had so much coffee during the night her stomach needed a caffeine break. Besides, tea was soothing and damn it, she needed to be soothed.

Or, at the very least, she told herself silently, commiserated with. Gripping the mug, she walked to the phone on the counter, picked up the receiver and hit number three on the speed dial. She sipped at her tea while the phone rang, then winced when Delilah's slurred voice demanded, "Who is crazy enough to be calling me at this hideous hour?"

"Sorry," Rose said quickly. "Really, sorry, Dee. I didn't even look at the time."

She did now, though, and cringed. Five o'clock in the morning. "Look, I'll talk to you later, okay? Go back to sleep."

"Sure," Dee said with a groan. "That's gonna happen. What's going on?"

"Have you got an hour or two?" Rose asked on a sigh. Before Dee could answer, though, she shook her head and said, "It's nothing that won't wait. We'll talk later. I can't do this on the phone, anyway. I'm really sorry."

"Rose!"

But she hung up, feeling as though she was batting a thousand. Sex with a client, followed by a big fight and ooh, maybe pregnant. And then finally, she'd awoken her best friend. Maybe she could find a puppy to kick and make everything perfect.

"Okay, that's it. You need to get out of this house for a while." She grabbed her bright pink sweatshirt off the back of a chair, picked her keys off a hook by the door and, carrying her tea with her, headed for the front door.

She stepped out into the damp, cold mist of the fog and a few steps from the house, she was lost in it.

Eight

Lucas was grateful to have somewhere else to focus his mind. He'd been up for hours, thinking over what had happened with Rose, and he needed a damn break before his brain exploded.

"You sure you want to do this now?"

Lucas turned off the engine and glanced at Sean. "Why wouldn't I?"

"I don't know," his brother said, taking a sip of his extra-large latte. "You look like you want to punch somebody, is all. And since I don't want it to be me and since if you punch Warren we could get sued, I just thought you might want to wait a while. Cool down from whatever's got your jets firing so hot."

"Well, you thought wrong," Lucas muttered.

"Okay, then," Sean said with a shrug. "Let's start the show."

They were at Long Beach harbor, not far from Terminal Island. Mostly, this area was filled with naval vessels and the cargo ships that sailed in and out of the harbor every day. The air was cold and smelled like fish and diesel oil.

It was almost six in the morning and people were already moving at the King Construction yard. The security guard at the gate had opened it for them the minute he recognized Lucas's SUV. Now the car was parked beside the warehouse-size building that stored the company's tools and machinery. Men and women—King Construction didn't discriminate against women on a work crew—moved around the building and surrounding yard, talking, laughing, getting their gear for whatever projects they were on.

Every morning, the working crews would come here, to the warehouse, to get what they needed for the jobs that started precisely at eight. A lot of construction firms didn't store their equipment in one central location. But the Kings figured it was easier to protect their investment in the tools this way and it gave all of their workers a chance to get to know each other. Friendships on a job site made the work go better.

And, Lucas told himself, this way he had known exactly where he could find Warren. Sure, he could have fired the man over the phone but that was damned impersonal. The least he owed someone who worked for him was a face-to-face when that job was ending.

"Hey, Sean!" someone called out. "Come on over here and settle a bet for me!"

Sean glanced at Lucas. "You handle this on your own?"

Rolling his eyes, Lucas snapped, "Yes, Mom. I think I can handle it."

"Without hitting him?"

"Go away, Sean."

"Right." Still, he gave Lucas another worried glance before moving off to where three of their crew were holding a loud debate over football.

Lucas shook his head, amused as he heard Sean jump right into the argument with an easy camaraderie. As good as he was with the tech stuff, Sean also was the most easygoing guy Lucas had ever known.

He put thoughts of his brother aside as he walked into the cavernous warehouse. Heavy thuds and clanks sounded and seemed to echo as the different crews loaded up what they would need for the day. The steel walls reverberated with the roar of one of the diesel engines and men shouted to each other to be heard over the noise.

It was a good sound, though. Lucas had always enjoyed being on a job site. Most of the time now, he worked on the phone from the office, but every once in a while, it was good to get back to the basics. Check in with their crews. And just as Rafe had only a few months ago, actually work a job. Though Rafe had done it because he had lost a bet, Lucas enjoyed working a job occasionally just to keep his hand in.

The tension in his shoulders eased a little as he let his surroundings soak in. Whatever else was going on in his life, here at King Construction, he knew exactly what he was doing.

He nodded at the people he passed, stopped to answer a question, then asked one of his own, "Julio, have you seen Warren around this morning?"

"Yeah." Julio Vega, about thirty-five with a thick black mustache and sharp brown eyes, lifted one arm and pointed toward the back of the warehouse, where the loaders and cement mixers were housed. "He's back there."

"Thanks." Lucas found his quarry easily enough then, but by the look on Warren's face when he saw Lucas, he was guessing this wasn't going to go well.

"Boss," the man said, with a brisk nod and a clenching of his jaw.

"Warren, we need to talk."

"If this is about the WeDig problem—"

"It is," Lucas told him, slapping one hand to the cold, metal side of the cement mixer. "You know, you were lucky that the only thing the men hit was a water pipe. It could have been a gas line. The whole damn neighborhood could have gone up in an explosion and fire."

Warren was in his forties, balding, with a full red beard. His face flushed, but it wasn't embarrassment coloring his features, it was anger. "*Could have* doesn't count. It wasn't the gas line, Lucas. Yeah, there was a damn flood, but we got the pumps in, most of the water's gone and we'll have the damage to the redwood deck repaired by end of the week."

Defensive. Lucas couldn't blame him but he also noticed that the man wasn't exactly apologizing, either. He knew damn well what might have happened and *could have* always counted. On a job site, there were so many things that could go wrong at any given moment, it was up to the man in charge to stay one step ahead of all problems.

"Yeah," Lucas said, keeping his voice even and his tone calm. "But doing all of that means we're *not* doing the job we were hired to do. Plus, we have to eat the cost of the repairs to the deck."

Shaking his head, he noticed the other man's temper

spiking, in the way his jaw muscles twitched and his hands continued to fist and relax at his sides. Warren could be as mad as he liked, but it was the wrong damn attitude to take with the boss when it was your own blasted mistake that had caused the mess in the first place.

"Warren, you know as well as I do, we lose money every day we spend correcting what went wrong on your site. Now we're behind on the job, which puts us behind on the *next* job." He patted the cement mixer, then folded his arms across his chest. "You were in charge, and you should have made sure WeDig cleared you before any of the guys so much as lifted a shovel."

Warren's barrel chest expanded with the huge gulp of air he took in. "You can't lay all of this off on me."

"Who else?" Lucas demanded, his own temper beginning to build. Hell, he knew mistakes happened— briefly, he thought about last night with Rose and could admit that he made mistakes, too—but he didn't have a bit of sympathy for someone so stubborn they couldn't even own up to it. "*You* were the foreman on the job."

"Every one of those guys has worked for you long enough to know better than to start digging," the man argued hotly. "Am I the babysitter, too?"

Warren's voice was getting louder, and Lucas heard other sounds in the warehouse quiet down. He knew people were listening and couldn't seem to care. He'd have preferred that he and Warren could settle this quietly, but maybe it was just as well that everyone here was reminded of the rules. The Kings believed in second chances, sure.

But *keep* screwing up and you're out.

"You're not the babysitter, Warren. You're the man who gives the orders on the site." His anger suddenly fading away into a mass of just-plain-tired, Lucas added, "This isn't the first time you've made mistakes on a job, either. King Construction has a solid reputation, and we'll do what we have to, to protect it."

"Like *fire* me?" Warren demanded. "That's what this is about, right? You came down here to fire me?"

"That's right," Lucas said flatly. He was done here. He'd said what he had to say and now he just wanted it finished. "I did. You'll get two weeks' severance, plus your vacation pay, but I want you off King property in the next half hour. One of the guards will walk you out."

"A guard? Now I'm a thief you have to follow around until I leave?"

"It's standard procedure, Warren, and you know it," Lucas told him.

"Standard procedure. That's great." Warren was clearly furious, but he was also surprised. Lucas saw it in his eyes. Apparently, he had expected the Kings to give him another warning and that would be the end of it. He backed up a step, muttered under his breath and ran one hand across the top of his bald head. Finally, he glared at Lucas. "Five years I've worked for you and you toss me aside this easy?"

And just like that, Lucas thought, his own anger was back. "Like I said, this wasn't your first mistake. And hell, I could even accept the mistakes if you'd just *once* taken responsibility for them. But no. You always push it off on the guys. Their fault. They didn't listen." Lucas took a breath and blew it out. "Well, Warren, when you're in charge, you better make damn sure they're listening to you."

"You son of a bitch. What am I supposed to do now?"

"No longer my problem," Lucas told him simply and started past him. His task was over and he didn't feel any better. Now he had to head back to the office and try to concentrate on work, when the reality was, he knew damn well Rose would be front and center in his mind all day—just as she had been all night.

"Don't you turn your back on me—" Warren reached out, grabbed Lucas's arm and spun him around. Drawing his right arm back, the man took a swing at him, but Lucas blocked the punch easily enough and threw one of his own into Warren's stomach that had him bending over and wheezing for air.

Irritated beyond belief, Lucas just glared at the man. "What the hell were you thinking? Throwing a swing at me? On top of being fired you want to be arrested?"

"You hit me."

"Yeah," Lucas said. "I told Sean I wouldn't, but you just couldn't help yourself, could you? Had to ratchet this up into a fight. You really are an idiot, aren't you?"

"I'll sue!" Warren managed to say, raising his furious gaze to Lucas.

"No, you won't," Julio said from right behind Lucas. "I saw the whole thing. You took the first punch. Lucas was defending himself."

Grateful, Lucas nodded at the younger man. A lawsuit would have been expensive and time-consuming. With Julio stepping forward, they'd avoid the hassle, and he appreciated it. "Julio, get security back here to escort Warren to his car."

Julio sent the still wheezing man a disgusted look, but nodded and said, "Right, boss."

Lucas moved away, still feeling a nagging sense of something unfinished inside him. Even hitting that moron hadn't helped any.

He walked out of the warehouse, oblivious to the noise, the laughter and conversation. The fog was burning off and the sun was a hazy, rising ball of fire overhead. He shoved his hands into his pockets, took a deep breath of the sea air and told himself that the real problem wasn't Warren, and he knew it.

It was Rose. How they'd left things.

When she'd walked out of his house last night it had taken everything in him not to go after her, carry her back into the house and tie her to his damn bed. He could still see the look of wild fury in her eyes when he had called her *Saint Rose*. And he remembered, too, that arguing with her had been as damned intoxicating as making love to her.

The woman was getting to him on so many levels he couldn't count them all.

So it was best that she'd left last night. And good that he hadn't spoken to her since. After all, he reminded himself sternly, this had been the plan. He'd gotten her into his bed. Now all he had to do was tell Dave all about it and then stop seeing Rose altogether. Perfect.

Except for the niggling question of whether or not they'd created a child. Gritting his teeth, Lucas reined in his thoughts and tucked them at the back of his mind, where no doubt they would continue to torture him all the damn day.

"You hit him, didn't you?" Sean asked when he strolled up alongside him.

"What?" Lucas turned and frowned at his brother. "How'd you know?"

"The guys are talking about it. You came off really well in the telling, by the way."

"That's just great," Lucas muttered. "Warren took the first swing, but yeah. I punched him."

Sean handed over his latte. "Here. Have some."

Lucas took a few long swallows, welcoming the caffeine before handing it back.

"I knew you'd hit him," Sean said with a shrug. "That's why I wanted to go in with you."

"To stop me?"

"Hell no," Sean said. "*I* wanted to hit him."

Reluctantly, Lucas grinned. No matter how screwed up his life was, it was still good to have brothers.

The knock at the front door came only a few minutes after Rose had returned from her predawn walk through the fog. She was still exhausted, still struggling with her thoughts and in no mood for company. She pulled back the edge of the curtains to peer out and sighed.

"Ready or not," she muttered, "company's here, and it's not going anywhere."

Her own fault, she told herself as she walked to the front door and unlocked it. If Rose hadn't called an hour ago, Dee wouldn't be standing on her front porch right now, with two lattes and a bag that hopefully included doughnuts.

She opened the door and gave her friend a half smile. "You didn't have to come over, you know."

"Right," Dee said, walking past her into the living room. "My best friend calls me at the crack of dear-God-why-am-I-awake, and I should just roll over and drop back into dreamland."

Wincing, Rose closed the front door, locked it and followed her friend into the small, cozy living room. Dee was already on the couch, her sandal-clad feet propped on the coffee table and the serving tray of lattes on the cushion beside her.

Even at six-something in the morning, Delilah James looked gorgeous. She wore a body-hugging pale yellow shirt tucked into skintight dark-wash blue jeans. Her red hair was styled and fluffed, her makeup was flawless and her green eyes were practically glowing with curiosity.

All in all, Rose thought sadly, as she walked to the couch in her baggy sweats and battered sneakers, she felt like the ugly stepsister next to the shining Cinderella.

"I hope there are doughnuts in that bag," she said as she took a seat on the opposite end of the couch.

"Am I breathing? Yes, there are doughnuts in the bag. And a latte with your name on it."

"Thanks."

"Skip the thank-yous and tell me what's going on." Dee took a sip of her own latte and waited. One of her best skills as a girlfriend was that she was a terrific listener.

Rose knew all too well that Delilah would sit right there on the couch all morning and into the afternoon if she had to, waiting for Rose to spill her guts. Then she would listen without judging—mostly—and after that, she would support whatever it was Rose decided to do.

If only she *knew* what to do.

"It's a long story," Rose said, taking a sip of the latte and letting its heat slide through her system like a blessing.

"I brought a lot of doughnuts," Dee pointed out. "So start talking."

Surrendering to the inevitable, Rose dug in the bag for a doughnut, took a healthy bite and started talking.

An hour later, she was stuffed full, her eyes were grittier than ever and she was more exhausted than she'd ever been in her life.

"So," Rose said on a sigh as she rummaged in the

now empty bag for the few remaining crumbs, "that's the story of my incredibly screwed-up life."

"It's a beauty of a story, I'll give you that," Dee said, taking the bag away to crumple it, ignoring Rose's frown. She tossed it onto the coffee table beside their empty latte cups. "The question is, what are you going to do now?"

"Heck if I know." Rose laid one hand on her flat belly and tried to imagine the reality of carrying a child.

An instant later, she was wishing for more dough-nuts.

"You're probably not pregnant," Dee said thought-fully. "I mean, people try for *years* without conceiving. What're the odds you could do it in one try?"

"True," she agreed, not really believing it.

"And I know you probably don't want to hear this, but as the best friend, I have to at least suggest it…"

"What?" she asked warily.

Dee sighed. "There is a pill you can take the morning after, and you know it."

"I know," Rose said. "I actually thought of that around three this morning." Then she shook her head. "But I can't, Dee. It would be like wishing the baby away—if there is one—and I couldn't live with it. With Mom and Dad both gone now, if there *is* a baby, it would be my family, you know? So I can't, you know? I mean, it's good that it's out there, but it's not for me."

"Yeah. Wouldn't be for me, either." Dee leaned over and patted Rose's hand in support. "So, we'll just have to hope for the best, and wait and see on the baby front. On the Lucas front…"

"Oh," Rose told her with a quick shake of her head, "trust me when I say there is no Lucas front."

"Please. You can't even sleep for thinking about the man."

"That doesn't mean there's anything there, Dee. It just means that we had one wild, incredible night of sex followed by a humiliating argument." She took a breath and blew it out again. "Saint Rose."

Dee laughed, and Rose sent her a look.

"Sorry," her friend said, making an effort to stop the chuckles. "But if you could see the look on your face when you said that."

Rose grabbed one of the throw pillows, tugged it out from behind her back and held it in front of her, wrapping both arms around it. "The Saint-Rose thing notwithstanding, you should have seen the expression on *Lucas's* face when he told me that we'd be getting married if I turn up pregnant. He meant every word, Dee."

"So what?" Dee scooted closer, draped one arm around Rose's shoulder and said, "He can't force you to marry him, sweetie. All he can do is bluster and demand. You don't have to do a damn thing you don't want to—beyond sharing custody, of course."

Rose dropped her head to the back of the couch and stared up at the ceiling. "Custody battles. Doesn't that sound like a good time?"

"You play, you pay," Dee told her gently.

"Isn't this the part where you're supposed to comfort me?"

"Right. Well, here's the comfort." Dee gave her shoulders a squeeze. "You're probably not pregnant, so chances are, you'll never have to see Lucas King again."

Never see Lucas again. Four words that left a cold,

dark empty feeling inside her. Rose looked at her friend. "Sadly, that thought isn't much comfort, either."

Dee nodded. "Yeah, I know."

Nine

After Dee left, Rose had a brief cry and a long nap, then woke up feeling almost human again. She still didn't have a clue what she was going to do next, but whatever it turned out to be, she was sure she could handle it. If she never saw Lucas again, at least she'd had that one night with him that she used to dream of experiencing.

Of course now, she would be dreaming *about* that night for the rest of her life, but that was okay, she thought firmly. She could deal.

"Hear that, universe? I can take it." She stirred a big pot of beef-and-barley soup and took a deep breath of the amazing scents wafting into the air.

Outside, it was dark, and a storm had blown in off the ocean. Wind rattled tree limbs and rain tapped at the windows like nervous fingers. But inside, all was warm and cozy.

Cooking had always soothed her. As a child, she remembered standing on a chair at the counter while the family cook taught her to make cookies. And as Rose got older, the lessons became more complex. By the time she was a teenager, she spent most of her spare time in the kitchen.

She hadn't had boyfriends—not with her father and brother standing guard over her. So she spent most nights alone in the house, coming up with new recipes to ease the boredom.

Now, Rose set the spoon down on the ceramic-duck spoon rest in the center of her stove and realized that she'd come full circle. Years later and here she was standing in her kitchen daydreaming about guys. Well, *one* guy.

"And that's just pitiful."

She took a seat at the kitchen table and reached for the dark green shirt she had left hanging over the back of one of the chairs. The shirt Lucas had loaned her the night before, she'd meant to wash it today, but hadn't. Lifting it to her face, she inhaled the scent of him and let pangs of regret and disappointment rush through her.

"No," she whispered, "*this* is pitiful."

God, she didn't know what was wrong with her. It wasn't as if she'd never had sex before. And fine, yes, there was the pregnancy worry hanging over her head, but that wasn't what was bothering her, either. Why was she so torn up inside? Why couldn't she take a deep breath without feeling as if there were iron bands around her lungs?

"And why are you asking yourself so many questions when you already know the answers?"

Her fingers trailed across the gold crown and the King Construction logo on the shirt. An image of Lucas sprang up in her mind—dark hair tumbled across his forehead. Blue eyes going hot with passion as he covered her body with his own. And Rose finally admitted to herself what the problem here really was.

She was in love with Lucas King. A part of her had loved him for three years, she thought, fingers still tracing across the King logo on his shirt. From the moment Dave had brought him home and she looked up into those blue eyes. He had been polite, a little distant—no doubt having gotten the off-limits warning from Dave already—but he had smiled at her and something inside Rose had come to life.

She'd been lost even back then.

Maybe that was why she had never found another man that made her heart race and her knees go weak. Maybe that was the real reason she'd agreed to marry Henry Porter when her family asked her to. Somewhere inside her, she had realized that she'd never have the man she wanted, so what did it matter?

Which had been a really bad reason to get married. But looking back, Rose knew she wouldn't have changed anything even if she could have.

Oh, her marriage had been awful—but in a weird way, it had also been good for her. She had changed a lot, thanks to Henry's being such a miserable husband. By the time that very brief marriage fizzled out, she had found the kind of courage and confidence she had always lacked before.

Without that sharp learning curve, Rose didn't know if she ever would have had the nerve to open her own business, let alone take a stand against her older brother. When their father died, Dave had stepped into the patriarchal role as if he'd been born to it…which, he really had, actually. But Rose had already grown too much to give him the kind of power over her their father had once claimed.

She smiled wistfully to herself, remembering the expression on Dave's face the first time she had said no to one of his orders. It had been well worth the jittering anxiety and the hot ball of tension in her stomach. It hadn't been easy to take that first step, but when she did, the world hadn't ended. Dave hadn't stopped loving her.

In fact, to give Dave his due, once she had set down ground rules and let him know that she wouldn't be bossed around for the rest of her life, he had actually backed off. Oh, he was still authoritarian, but half the time she didn't listen and he didn't really expect her to anymore.

Which was a victory of sorts, wasn't it?

But Lucas…he was a different matter. She could still see him in his bedroom, glaring at her as he told her that if she were pregnant, they'd be getting married, like it or not.

Resentment jumped into life inside her. She straightened up in the chair and unconsciously squared her shoulders. Rose wouldn't trade one bossy man for another. She wouldn't stand her ground against her brother and then cave for Lucas.

Rose had already done marriage for the wrong reasons. The next time she said *I do,* it would be because she was madly in love—and loved just as fiercely in return. She wouldn't accept less and if she did turn out to be pregnant, she certainly wouldn't marry him just because of their child.

Her mind racing with arguments she couldn't use because Lucas wasn't there, Rose couldn't sit still another minute. Dropping the shirt on the chair back again, she got up and walked out to the living room.

Mindlessly, she straightened the already tidy room, fluffing pillows, stacking magazines on the corner of the coffee table. She could have turned on the stereo for company, but her thoughts were already so busy, she didn't need the extra distraction. A little silence, she told herself, was probably just what she needed. She should have known it wouldn't last.

When the doorbell rang, she jumped and whirled around. Her silly heart raced suddenly as her first thought was that Lucas was there. But in the next instant, that hope died.

"Rose!" her brother called out, hitting the doorbell again just for good measure. "Rose! I know you're home. I see your skillet car in the driveway."

Just what she needed, she thought, the other hard-headed man in her life. Hurrying to the door, she threw it open and instantly, wind-driven rain slapped at her with icy needles of wet. "Dave, what're you doing here?"

"Nice to see you, too, sis." He bent down and briefly kissed her forehead before walking past her into the house. He shook his head, swiped one hand through his wet hair and asked, "Wow, what smells so good?"

Rose sighed. Looked like she would be having company for dinner. "Beef-and-barley soup."

He looked at her and his eyebrows lifted. "Home-made?"

She had to smile at his hopeful expression. "Of course. You want some?"

"That'd be great." He shrugged out of his jacket and hung it on one of the hooks behind her front door. As he followed her to the kitchen, he kept up a running monologue. "This storm's got lousy timing. I've got a crew out on Pacific Coast Highway trying to shore up a retaining wall before the rain gets too bad. There's a mud hole where another family's new den was going to be and I've been out at a site helping the crew tack plastic up on a torn-off roof before the house flooded. The rain caught everybody by surprise."

Rain clattered at the windows, and the wind moaned as it swept under the eaves of Rose's old bungalow. The lights in the kitchen were bright against the dark, and the scent of the bubbling soup welcomed them into the room.

"Did you get the roof covered?"

"Yeah, but it was close," he said, scrubbing both hands over his face as if trying to rub away the memory. "We're putting in a second story, so we had the tarps ready to go—they just had to go up a lot faster than we thought. And did you notice? Not one damn weatherman predicted this storm?"

Rose was used to hearing construction stories. She'd grown up on them. And usually, Southern California weather cooperated nicely with builders. But every once in a while...

"Sounds like you've had a busy day," she said, going directly to a cabinet and taking down two soup bowls. She grabbed spoons from a drawer and carried them to the narrow table. Then taking the bowls to the stove, she filled each of them with the soup that had been simmering most of the afternoon.

"Busier than I'd like," Dave admitted, arms braced on her narrow table. "What about you?"

"Hmm?"

"Haven't talked to you in a couple of weeks, so thought I'd stop by and—"

"Get dinner?" Rose finished for him as she carried the steaming bowls of soup to the table.

He grinned, and she couldn't help returning his smile. She loved her brother. She really did. Rose just wished they had the kind of relationship that would allow her to tell him what was happening in her life. But not only could she not talk to Dave about a man, she also knew only too well how he would react to the mention of Lucas King. She just wished she knew why.

Dave pulled one of the four chairs out for her to sit down and that's when he spotted the green T-shirt.

Rose held her breath and then made a grab for the shirt before he could get a good look at it. But Dave was faster. He held it up and immediately saw it was a man's shirt.

"So who's the guy, Rose?" he asked, smiling at her in a way that made her think this might turn out all right after all. "Is he a secret? Because as the big brother, I should be able to check him out before you get too attached. Make sure he's good enough for my baby sister."

"Dave…"

Rose knew the moment Dave spotted the logo. Her stomach sank as her brother's eyes frosted over and all semblance of a teasing smile slipped away.

"King Construction?" He stood up, still staring at the gold crown on the green shirt crumpled in his fist. "Is this some kind of joke?"

"No," Rose said on a sigh as she tugged the shirt out of his grasp. So much for a touching brother-sister bonding moment. "It's my private life and it's none of your business, Dave."

He stalked the short distance to the kitchen sink, turned around and stomped right back again. Glaring at her, he argued, "The hell it's not. One of the Kings has been here. And left his *shirt*."

"He wasn't here," Rose said tightly. "I went to his house. I...spilled something and had to borrow one of his shirts."

"Uh-huh." He crossed his arms over his chest and braced his feet wide apart. "And why were you at his house?"

"Cooking lessons." Rose threw both hands high, realized she was waving the shirt around like a red flag in front of a bull and tossed it to the counter behind her. "It's what I do, remember? He hired me to teach him to cook."

"Sure he did." Dave shook his head fiercely, and his mouth worked as if there were dozens of words clogged up inside him that he wouldn't set free. He looked disgusted, worried and furious all at once. "Which one?" he said flatly. "Which King?"

Here it comes, she told herself. The argument of the century was about to get started.

Lifting her chin, she folded her arms over her chest, too, in a perfect imitation of his stance. Locking her gaze with his, she said simply, "Lucas."

Astonishment filled his eyes and had his mouth dropping open. "Are you serious? Lucas King? Damn it, Rose! Why him?"

"Why not him, Dave?" she demanded. "You and Lucas used to be friends. Then you weren't, and I never knew why."

"You didn't have to know," he muttered, turning away from her to walk to the closest window. He braced his hands on the wall at either side of the glass and stared out at the rain-splotched night beyond.

Rose could see her brother's reflection in the glass,

and she felt a twinge of sympathy at the taut misery etched into his features. But that didn't change the fact that it was past time for him to tell her the truth. What was the awful secret that had destroyed his friendship with Lucas? Why was the mere mention of the King name enough to shift Dave into defensive mode?

"I need to know now, Dave," she said quietly, her words dropping into the silence like stones into a well.

"Why?" he asked just as quietly. "Why can't you just take my word on it and stay away from the Kings? Especially Lucas?"

She took a breath and let it go on a sigh. "It's too late for that."

He turned around then and looked at her, hard and long. She held his gaze and when she saw the unmistakable question in his eyes, she nodded. "That bastard slept with you?"

"I slept with him, too. So if you're going to be mad…"

Defeated, Dave's shoulders slumped and he muttered, "Damn it, Rose, not Lucas."

"Talk to me. Tell me what went wrong," she said, laying one hand on her brother's arm.

Absently, he gave her hand a pat, then turned away again, apparently not able to meet her gaze while he talked. "You're right. You should know. Maybe if I'd been honest about this before, you would have kept your distance."

"Just tell me," she repeated.

"I paid one of the King assistants for insider information, and I used that information to undercut their bids on jobs." Finally, he turned back around to look at her. "Basically, I stole from the Kings."

Staggered, Rose could only stare at the man she had thought she knew. "I don't believe this. Why?"

Sighing, Dave dropped into his chair again. "I have excuses. Reasons. Dad was sick, jobs were in short supply, we needed the money. We invested in a few bad deals and took a beating." He braced his elbows on his thighs. "There were hospital bills, payrolls to be met and…like I said. I have excuses. But the bottom line is, I stole from Lucas. My friend."

"He knew?" Rose asked, slumping into the chair beside her brother's. Of course he knew, she told herself. Why else would Lucas's features freeze up at the mention of his old friend's name?

"He guessed," Dave told her, looking into her eyes. "He couldn't prove it. No evidence. But yeah, he knows."

Rose was so shaken she didn't know what to say. Or think. Her brother was a thief, and the man she loved was his victim. And to think that just a few hours ago, she had thought her life was as complicated as it could possibly get.

"Why didn't he say anything?" she whispered. "I mean, I get why you didn't, but why would Lucas keep quiet?"

"Like I said, no evidence. And without that, if he made accusations, he'd just look like a poor loser." Dave blew out a breath and reached over to take her hand. "Rose, has it occurred to you that Lucas hired you and then romanced you not because he wanted you, but for revenge on me?"

"No." She tugged her hand free of her brother's and jumped to her feet. Walking across the room, she slapped both hands palm down onto the counter and felt the cold of the granite seep into her skin. "He wouldn't."

"You're sure about that?"

She shot Dave a look as he stood up and came toward her. "Yes. Lucas wouldn't have—he never would have…" Her words trailed off as her mind and heart began a silent battle.

Her brain insisted that Dave was right. Why else would a man like Lucas King be interested in "Saint Rose," but for revenge? But her heart and body remembered every stroke of his hands, every kiss, every whispered word of passion and heat and would not believe that none of it had been real.

The storm pelted Long Beach for three days.

By the third day, Lucas was like a tiger in a too-small cage. He couldn't get out to a job site because of the rain, and if he had to sit in the damn office and calm down one more client, his head was going to explode.

That afternoon, he got in his car and started driving. As if on automatic pilot, his SUV took him directly to Rose's house. She hadn't been hard to find. All he'd had to do was look up the name of her business and there she was.

Now he sat outside the tiny, sky-blue bungalow, listening to the rain beat against the roof of his car. She was inside, he knew. The skillet car was in the driveway. A reluctant smile curved his mouth as he looked at the ridiculous thing. Only Rose would drive that car. And only Rose could have turned him inside out as she had.

For days, all he'd been able to do was think about her. He saw her in his sleep. Caught traces of her scent in his kitchen and every time he lay down on his bed, he wanted to reach out and find her there. He'd actually come to care about Rose.

Which told him it was time to end this.

His plan had worked fine, so it was done. He wasn't looking for a relationship. Wasn't the marrying kind and if he was, he sure as hell wouldn't be marrying into

Dave Clancy's family. So there was no point in leaving things between he and Rose up in the air. It was time to cut and run.

If it turned out she was pregnant, he'd worry about it then.

Getting out of the car, he walked slowly through the driving rain, his gaze fixed on the windows where lamplight played behind sheer curtains. Before he made it to the front porch, the door opened and Rose was standing on the threshold, watching him.

Everything in him eased as his gaze moved over her. Her blond hair was loose around her shoulders, and she wore faded blue jeans and a scoop-necked red blouse that displayed just the tops of her full breasts. Her eyes were guarded and she had such a tight grip on the door that her knuckles were white.

"Lucas."

"Hi."

"You're soaked."

"What?" He glanced up at the sky as if surprised to find himself getting wet. "Yeah. Guess I am."

She stepped back, farther into the house. "You want to come in?"

He nodded and took the steps in one long stride. Then he was brushing past her, his upper arm sliding across her breasts as he walked into her house. The jolt of heat from that minor touch of their bodies stayed with him as he peeled off his jacket and handed it to her. She hung it on a hook and then stood there, staring up at him.

Waiting.

Everything in him wanted to grab her. To forget about his plan. To forget about Dave and revenge and anything else that wasn't as real as she was. But that wasn't why he was here.

He followed after her, not much caring for the stiff formality that was suddenly between them. She led him down a short hall into the smallest living room he'd ever seen.

Stepping into that room, he felt like Gulliver. Everything was too small for him. The couch, the chairs, the tables. The walls were covered in framed posters and a few family photos and the scent of something amazing was coming from the kitchen.

It was warm and cozy and he felt like the intruder he was. There was no welcome for him here. Clearly, he didn't belong and judging from the chill of her reception, he wouldn't be staying long, either. The sting of that thought vanished when he told himself that was how he wanted it, anyway.

When Rose turned to look at him, her eyes were dry, but there were shadows in those blue depths that bothered him more than he wanted to admit.

"Why are you here, Lucas?"

Good question. He'd come to say goodbye, but now all he wanted to do was reach for her. He fisted his hands at his sides to keep from giving in to that urge.

Lucas looked at her, and, for the first time, noticed that she appeared to be nervous. Uneasy. Hell, maybe the last few days had been hard on her, too. They'd left too many things in the air that night. Too many things unsaid. And there was still a major question hanging over both of their heads. No wonder she looked as ragged as he felt.

She'd probably be as grateful as he would to have the unfinished business between them straightened up. To make a clean break. "Look, I only came to say that I won't be seeing you again."

"Is that right?"

Not a flicker of emotion showed on her features, and Rose, he had already learned, wasn't a woman to hide from what she was feeling. Her laughter was always genuine and her anger just as up-front and easily recognizable. But right now, she looked…empty. As if she'd been drained of all emotion and left to deal with a hollow sensation inside, like the one he'd been carrying around in his chest the last few days.

He frowned, not caring for that image, but he kept talking, wanting to make himself clear. He had to make her understand that whatever there had been between them was now over. And maybe then, they could both just put the past couple of weeks behind them. "I won't be needing any more cooking lessons, either."

"I see."

His scowl went deeper. Damn it, didn't she feel a thing? He was having a hard time saying this, the least she could do was look as though it mattered to her. "It's nothing against you, Rose. I just don't see how anything good can come from what's between us."

"Right. Of course not."

Again, her words were flat, her eyes cool and distant.

"What the hell is wrong with you?" he blurted out, wondering where the woman he knew had gone. This woman—detached, aloof—was someone he didn't even recognize. Reaching out to her, he went to grab her shoulders, but she took a hasty step to the side, avoiding his touch. "Rose, what's going on?"

"You tell me," she said quietly, her gaze locked with his. "The reason you won't be seeing me again…is it because my brother stole from you?"

Stunned, Lucas felt her words like a blow to the chest. How… He stared at her, hardly able to process this. The only way she could have found out that information was from her brother. "Dave told you?"

"So it's true," she whispered, shifting her gaze from his as if she just couldn't look at him any longer. Scraping her hands up and down her arms, she added, "Yes. Dave told me."

This he hadn't expected. Who knew that Dave would finally come clean? After two years of keeping his silence, what had pushed him into a confession? To Rose, of all people? And if her brother and she had been talking, did that mean that Dave knew about Lucas and Rose?

Grinding his teeth against the anger and frustration pumping through him, he asked, "Did you tell your brother about us?"

"Why?" she asked, now wrapping her arms around her middle as if needing something to hold on to, even if it was only herself. "Was that a secret, too?"

He tried not to hear the pain she was finally allowing to show in her voice. He still had to know, so he asked again. "Did you tell him?"

"He guessed," she said on a tired sigh. "He saw your shirt. The one you gave me the other night."

"Great. That's great." Shaking his head, he felt the last of his plan shatter out from under him. He'd thought he had it all figured out. The perfect revenge. Now it was all gone, and he was left standing alone with the woman he'd dragged into the rubble.

He pushed one hand through his hair and tried to figure out how this could have gone any worse, but he didn't come up with anything.

"Now I need to know something from you," Rose said.

His gaze snapped to hers. "What?"

"Was Dave right? He said you were only with me to get back at him. Was this all for revenge?"

He hadn't planned to tell Rose about the revenge plot. He wasn't interested in hurting *her,* after all. It was Dave he wanted to make pay. But looking into her eyes, he couldn't lie to her, either. There'd already been enough lies between them. "Yeah. That was the plan."

"The *plan.*" She huffed out a breath and shook her head again. "Wow. There was an actual plan."

Her cool blue eyes locked on him, and Lucas shifted uncomfortably under that steady regard. It had been a long time, years maybe, since he'd felt the stirrings of guilt and regret that were starting to burn through him right now. He couldn't even remember the last time he'd felt like this.

And he didn't like it. Damn it, he had done what needed doing. Dave had had to pay for his betrayal, and now he would. Collateral damage wasn't pretty, but sometimes it was unavoidable.

Going for a bravado he wasn't really feeling, Lucas said, "Rose, I didn't set out to hurt *you.*"

She nodded jerkily as if she were a puppet having her strings yanked. "So, just a bonus for you, then."

Another sharp stab of something hot and painful poked at his insides. He looked at her and felt completely torn. She was the sister of the man he considered his enemy. But she was also the woman he had spent the last couple of weeks with, laughing. Talking. *Loving.*

No. He pushed that last word out of his mind so fast, it was really nothing more than a blur on his consciousness. He didn't love Rose. He didn't love anyone. What he felt for her was…hell, he couldn't even name it, but he knew it wasn't love. How could it be?

That wasn't part of the plan.

He took a breath. "This wasn't how it was supposed to turn out."

"Really? Then what? You were just supposed to get me into bed and then you would disappear? Never to be heard from again? Was that it?"

"Pretty much," he admitted, though the words tasted bitter and had to be forced from his throat. When he'd first come up with this scenario, it had seemed pretty straightforward. Now, it was all tangled up in things he didn't want to identify. Now, he was looking into a pair of blue eyes glittering with pain and humiliation and he felt like kicking his own ass.

She was still staring at him as if he were a stranger that had somehow wandered into her home, so he tried to make her see this from his side. "Rose, I didn't know you when this started."

"You still don't, if you think I'm going to stand here and listen to you try to explain away what you did."

Frustration boiled through the regret. "Dave stole from me. Betrayed my friendship."

"And what have you done, Lucas? Is it really so different?" She glared at him for a long minute before looking away and adding, "At least Dave had a reason for what he did, all you had was your own petty need for payback."

"Petty?" He grabbed her shoulders and turned her to face him.

Fine, he deserved to feel like a jerk for using her. He could accept that. But damned if he'd stand there and have her tell him that his need for revenge was nothing more than petty. "I *trusted* him. My brothers trusted him. He turned on all of us. I don't think it's petty to want some satisfaction for that."

She pulled away from his touch, and instantly, his hands felt cold and empty.

"And I was a tool to be used."

"Not just a tool, Rose," he said, hating the words as they came out of his mouth, but somehow, he was unable to stop them. "You were—"

"Pitifully easy to trick?" she finished for him.

"Rose, try to understand," he said, even knowing that she wasn't listening to him anymore.

He reached out to her again, but she jerked back as if protecting herself from something foul.

Which, he thought, was just about right.

"Don't touch me," she said, shaking her head and swallowing hard. "God, you're just like all the rest of them. You used me. Like my father. And Dave. And Henry. My God, I didn't see it."

She laughed, and it was a harsh, brittle sound that tore at something inside Lucas that he refused to recognize.

"You weren't supposed to see it," he said.

"Well then, big congrats to you! Mission accomplished! Saint Rose taken down a peg, and big bad thief taught a very important lesson, I'm sure."

"Look, Rose—"

"No. *You* look," she interrupted, anger churning in her voice now and fury coloring her porcelain cheeks. "Whatever was between us? You're right. That's over. You got what you wanted, so we don't ever have to see each other again."

He didn't like the sound of that even though he'd gone to her house to pretty much say the same damn thing. And that didn't make a bit of sense. Lucas didn't like confusion. He liked order. He liked knowing where he was going, how he was going to get there and what he'd find when he arrived.

But ever since getting involved with Rose, he'd been wandering around in a daze. Why was he only noticing that now?

"Get out, Lucas. Get out of my house."

She was looking up at him as if he were the enemy. He guessed he'd earned that. He'd never been tossed out of a house before, but he supposed that he'd earned that, as well.

But he wasn't leaving until she understood one more thing.

"I'll go," he told her. "But we're not completely done until we know if you're pregnant or not. And if you are, Rose, I'll be back."

Ten

"He sent me a *check*."

Three days of silence, Rose told herself. No contact at all from Lucas and this is what she gets in the mail?

In the *mail*?

"How big a check?" Dee asked from her usual perch on the couch. Like the true best friend she was, Delilah had shown up a few hours ago with more lattes and, even more importantly, a fresh supply of doughnuts.

They'd spent the afternoon on the couch with Rose alternately feeling sorry for herself and wanting to go kick Lucas. Now, evening was crouched outside the windows and the rain was beginning again. It was as if the weather matched her mood lately. Southern California was getting the rainiest winter in twenty years, and Rose felt right at home in the gloom.

"How much is the check?" Delilah asked again.

"Does it matter?" Rose turned to look at her friend.

"For three days, I've been moping around here, missing that big ape, torturing myself and what does he do? He mails me a check for..." She glanced down and her eyes bugged out. *"Ten thousand dollars!"*

"Seriously?" Delilah bolted off the couch and snatched the check from Rose's numb fingers.

Even though she and Delilah had both been born into wealthy families, they had each been on their own for the last few years. Rose by choice; Delilah because her father had lost everything to the IRS. So ten thousand dollars seemed like a vast amount of money to both of them.

Which to Rose's mind only made this more insulting.

While her friend cooed over all the zeroes on the check, Rose's brain went into overdrive. Since the night she had practically thrown Lucas out of her house, she'd been miserable. Every minute, she'd ached for him— despite knowing that he'd been using her all along to get back at her brother.

What kind of sense did that make? Shouldn't love be more like a faucet? Turn it on when it was right and shut it off when it wasn't? She hadn't slept, had cried so much her eyes were no doubt permanently red and puffy and *this* is the thanks she got?

The universe had to kick her while she was down?

Was he really that cold? Had she romanticized every feeling she had about him? Rose swallowed hard and tried to look away from the offending piece of paper, but her gaze refused to shift. It was all there, her mind whispered. All the proof she needed that he had never cared. That every word, every touch between them had been a lie.

And what had the last few days been like for him? Was he out partying? Moving on to some bimbo who wouldn't care what he thought or said or did? Had he even given her a moment's thought aside from the time it had taken for him to write that stupid, insulting *check?*

"Ten thousand dollars," Delilah said. "'For services rendered.' Uh-oh."

"What? Services?" Rose grabbed the check so she could scowl down at Lucas's scrawled signature. That's when she saw the memo line. Delilah was right. *For services rendered.*

Her jaw dropped and her eyes widened even further than they had before. *"Services?"*

"Rose," Delilah said cautiously, "you know he meant the cooking lessons."

"Do I?" she snapped in a voice so high it cracked as fury rushed through every inch of her body like an out-of-control wildfire. She was practically vibrating she was so angry. And insulted again. And hurt. And humiliated.

"That no-good, lying…" She ran out of invectives when Delilah interrupted her.

"You know he's not paying you for sex."

"We don't know that," Rose told her, still so angry she could hardly draw a breath. "This was probably part of his 'plan.' The big goodbye speech after using me to get back at Dave, followed by a nice check—not too big, not too small. Payoff has to be handled carefully, after all.…"

"Oh, boy," Delilah muttered warily.

Rose hardly heard her. Her blood was rushing in her ears and her heartbeat was pounding as if she'd just completed a marathon. "Who does he think he is, anyway?"

"Rose…"

Her fingers curled into the check, and it was only

through a supreme act of control she didn't tear it into bits. Lucas King had given her a metaphorical slap for the last time. It was her turn now and she had a few things she wanted to say to him. In person.

She glared down at his signature again. "Think you can pay me off without even facing me over it? Well, I don't want your damn money."

"Let's not be hasty," Delilah urged.

"No," Rose said with a sharp nod. "You're right. I do want his money. But only what he owed me for those cooking lessons."

"He did say he was going to pay you three times your usual rate."

"That still wouldn't be ten thousand dollars, Dee," she said, tapping the edge of the check against her fingertips. "No, he did this on purpose. He sent a check that isn't so large I'd have to kill him, but still big enough for me to understand this was the big goodbye."

"There are worse ways to break up," Dee muttered.

"Hah! What? They were out of trinkets at the jewelry store?"

Delilah sighed. "You're going to go see him, aren't you?"

"You're damn right I am," Rose said, with a glint in her eye and a lift of her chin. Lucas King may have started all this with his ridiculous plan, but she was going to finish it. He wanted a big goodbye? Fine. She'd give him one. And when she was finished, he'd be sorry he had ever heard of Rose Clancy.

"Okay, as the best friend," Dee said cautiously, "I feel it's my duty to remind you that you actually *love* this guy, Rose. Remember the misery? The doughnuts? You're angry right now, but you still love him in spite of everything."

"I know," Rose said, pulling in one deep breath after another. "And *because* I love that big creep, there is just no way I'm letting him get away with this."

"Uh-huh," Dee said, "and then what?"

"Then," Rose told her firmly, "I will come home and do deep meditations or something until I'm *out* of love with him."

"Yeah, that'll work."

"Supportive. That's your job, remember?"

"Right, right." Delilah held up both hands. "I'm supporto girl. Need a getaway driver? Here I am. But Rose, there's still the question of whether or not you're pregnant to consider, too."

"I know." She nodded again, glanced at her flat belly and wondered for the thousandth time in the last few days if there was a baby already growing inside her. And if there was, that baby deserved better than a mother who was crazy and a father who didn't have the sense to know what was good for him.

Her shoulders slumped as her fingers moved over Lucas's handwriting. Shaking her head, she said, "If I am pregnant, I'll have to deal with Lucas. But if I let this go…him treating me like a bill to be paid…then how will we ever work together to take care of a baby? He may not love me, Dee. But he has to at least *respect* me."

Delilah nodded and gave her a smile. "You're absolutely right. I'm with you. Do you want me to go with you to see him?"

"No." Rose threw a look at the window and the cold, rainy day outside. "I have to do this alone."

"Okay, then." Delilah picked up her purse off the coffee table and shrugged into her windbreaker, pulling the hood up over her perfectly styled red hair. "But call me when it's over, okay?"

"I will." She stood there in the center of the living room and watched her friend leave. Then she told herself to get a firm grip on her sweeping emotions. There was no point in facing down Lucas if she couldn't calmly and clearly tell him exactly what she thought of him and his stupid check.

Minutes passed and she realized she wasn't going to calm down. The best she could hope for was that she wouldn't shriek at him or maybe kick him in the shins.

"Did he really think I could be bought off?" she asked herself, and then in the next instant, answered her own question. "Well, why wouldn't he? He knew Dave stole jobs out from under him, so in the world according to Lucas King, that makes all of the Clancys thieves."

Turning on her heel, she headed for her bedroom. She needed to change. And fix her hair. And makeup. *This* Clancy was going to teach Lucas King a lesson he wouldn't forget.

If it was the last thing she ever did for him.

"Lucas…"

He didn't even look up from his desk. "Evelyn, if you don't want Katie's cookies in the break room, tell Rafe."

"This isn't about the cookies," his secretary said and waited for him to look up at her. "Someone's here to see you."

Someone? Evelyn usually wasn't so vague. He frowned, then understood as a man walked up behind Evelyn, then slipped into Lucas's office. "Dave."

Almost the last person he'd expected to see here at King Construction. The only way he could have been more surprised was if Rose had shown up unannounced. Something inside him jolted to life at the thought, and he ruthlessly squashed it down.

He and Rose were over.

Even if he hadn't called an end to it himself, after the way things had gone between them at her house, he knew she was done with him.

He didn't like it and maybe he regretted the whole useless revenge plan in the first place—regretted it more than he would ever have thought possible—but hindsight was pretty much useless in most situations.

"It's okay, Evelyn," he said, standing up from behind his desk. He looked at the man opposite him and realized that he didn't even feel the old anger anymore.

Lucas couldn't help thinking about what Rafe and Sean had said, about letting it go. And somewhere over the last couple of days, he now realized, he *had*. Wasn't sure why. Wasn't even sure how. But that hard, cold ball he'd been carrying around in his gut for the past two years was finally gone.

When his secretary left and closed the door, Dave said simply, "You shouldn't have gone for Rose, Lucas."

There was that sting of shame again. But he didn't owe Dave anything, so he squashed that emotion flat. "And you shouldn't have betrayed our friendship, Dave."

"Damn it," Dave countered, "this was between you and me. You didn't have to drag my sister into it."

"Wrong." Lucas met his stare evenly. "This was between our *families*. You didn't just cheat me, Dave. You cheated my brothers. You cost us seven jobs that winter."

"Yeah," he said on a snort of self-derision. Scrubbing one hand across his face, Dave said, "I know. Still can't believe it myself, really. And you should know, I didn't want to do it."

"Small consolation. Whether you wanted to or not, you *did*."

"I needed the money," his old friend snapped, shooting Lucas a look that mixed both pride and embarrassment.

It was an admission he hadn't expected to hear. Hell, the Clancy family wasn't as wealthy as the Kings, but they came damn close. "For what? What was so damn important?"

Was he finally going to get the answers to the questions that had plagued him? And when he had them, would it make any difference?

Lucas had spent far too much time over the past two years thinking about the betrayal that had cut him so deeply. He'd even questioned his own ability as a judge of character and that bothered him more than anything. If he could be so wrong about Dave, what was to say he wasn't wrong about a lot of other people in his life?

"My father was dying, and the business was going down," Dave said, his words spilling from him as though a dam inside him had finally broken. He looked at Lucas. "Dad had made some bad investments in the years before I took over. He lost most of our capital. There were suppliers to be paid, contracts to honor and hospital bills piling up. I had to make good on it all or we would have lost everything we had left. I needed the jobs, Lucas." He scowled at the memories, but added, "I had to protect my family. I'm not sorry I was able to do that, but I am sorry I used you to do it."

Lucas could look at his old friend and see what that confession had cost him. He could even understand now, why Dave had done what he had. After all, there weren't many things Lucas wouldn't be willing to do to protect his brothers. So now that he knew the truth, how could he hold it against the man?

"You should've told me," he said finally. "We were friends. I could have helped you out, and you wouldn't have had to do what you did."

"Sounds good now." Dave laughed shortly and shook his head. "I couldn't tell you, Lucas. Pride's the one thing you and I always had in common. And that pride made me steal from a friend rather than admit that I was about to lose the company my grandfather built. Hell, I didn't even want to admit the truth to myself."

Rain slapped at the window behind him, the only sound in the room as the two men looked at each other and each tried to finally put the past behind them. Absently, Lucas wondered if fate hadn't taken a hand in the weather lately. If not for this new storm, Lucas would have been out inspecting the latest job site, talking to the crews. But with the weather delay, he had spent all afternoon in the office, catching up on paperwork. So he'd been here to hash this out with Dave.

Maybe this was fate's way of telling him just what his brothers had. Let it go.

"I was sorry to hear it when your dad died," he said quietly, offering the olive branch that they both needed.

"Thanks." Dave met his gaze and nodded. "I appreciate that. And I know that this doesn't mean we're friends again or anything."

"Not yet," Lucas admitted, though he was willing to scratch Dave off his active enemies list.

"What I came here to say isn't going to help that any, either," Dave told him. "You shouldn't have used my sister, Lucas. You had problems with me, I get that.

But you and I both know you went after her to stick it to me."

"Rose isn't up for discussion," Lucas said shortly. He was willing to forgive Dave for the stealing and the betrayal. But he wasn't going to stand here and talk about the woman he'd slept with to her brother.

Which struck him as odd, since telling Dave about sleeping with Rose had been the whole point of this exercise.

"The hell she's not," Dave countered, leaning both hands on Lucas's desk. "She's not like the women you usually hook up with."

"What do you know about that? I haven't even spoken to you in two years."

"Some things don't change."

Lucas gritted his teeth to keep from saying something he'd regret. Instead, he just stared into Dave's eyes, not giving an inch.

"Or do they?" Dave asked, a half smile on his face. "She got to you, didn't she? You thought you'd use Rose and walk away without a backward glance, but it wasn't as easy as you thought it would be, was it?"

He was right, damn it. About all of it. Lucas hadn't been able to slice Rose out of his mind or his soul. She was in there, deep, whether he wanted it or not. But he wasn't going to tell Dave that. "Stop now. I'm not talking about her with you."

"Fine, then just listen." Dave pushed off the desk. "Don't mess with her head, Lucas. If you're really finished then stay the hell away from her. Because if you hurt her again…you and I are going to go a few rounds."

With that, Dave walked out of his office. Alone, Lucas stared blindly at the closed door. He didn't like taking orders. Never had. But he couldn't blame Dave for this one.

Lucas didn't know what to feel anymore. For two years, he'd been carrying around what felt like a boulder, and now it was gone. A simple, five-minute conversation with Dave Clancy and he had a truce of sorts with his former friend.

All it had cost him was Rose.

Bull, his mind corrected instantly. Rose had never been his and so he couldn't have lost her. But even as he thought that, an image of her face as she stared him down that last night at her house loomed in his mind, taunting him. Even when her eyes had been spitting fire at him, he'd wanted her. Even now, he wanted her, he admitted.

Which meant exactly nothing, he assured himself.

Rose had been a temporary thing. Sure, she was still in his mind and his body was still fantasizing about her. But that was only because she was new. In a few weeks, he'd be over her. And as long as she wasn't pregnant, they'd never have to see each other.

She had been a means to an end and that end had now been completed. Story over.

Absently, he rubbed one hand over his chest, trying to soothe the heavy feeling centered there. But it didn't help.

Nothing helped.

"All right, enough," he muttered and stalked to the closet to grab the battered, brown leather jacket hanging inside. He shrugged it on, threw his office door open and walked out. "I'm leaving, Evelyn."

"Wow, and before seven, too," she said, but Lucas just kept walking.

There were far too many clever women in his life.

Eleven

It had finally stopped raining. Rose was cold. And wet. What she wanted to do was be home, curled up on her couch with a cup of hot tea in her hands and a mindless program on TV shattering the silence.

But she was determined to stay put until Lucas finally showed up at his house. For what had to be the tenth time, Rose checked her wristwatch again. A little after six. Why was he late?

When they had their cooking lessons together he was always here before now. Irritation gave way to worry.

Her gaze fixed on the rain-slicked surface of Ocean Boulevard and the cars flying past, fan-tails of water flying out behind them. Californians were notorious for forgetting how to drive on rainy streets from one year to the next. There were always more accidents during a storm.

Sitting in one of the Adirondack chairs on Lucas's

porch, she gripped her hands together in her lap and tried not to imagine his car as a twisted hunk of metal.

"Okay, don't be crazy," she murmured. "He's fine. He's just not home. Probably on a date or something. With some rich, gorgeous…"

Nope, don't go there, either, she told herself firmly.

She shouldn't care. Rose knew that. Lucas had lied to her, used her and then tossed her aside as soon as he was finished. She couldn't really blame him for seducing her, since she was pretty much in on that as well. But for the rest…she patted her shoulder bag, where his check was tucked away, and that alone stiffened her spine.

"Who're you?"

A deep voice splintered her thoughts and she looked up to see a bald, burly man with a full red beard standing in the middle of the lawn. He looked big, angry and, if she wasn't mistaken, very drunk. His eyes were narrowed on her. He was soaking wet and swaying on his feet.

A trickle of fear spilled down her spine.

Carefully, she reached into her purse and pulled her phone out.

"Where's Lucas?" the man demanded, taking a halting step toward her.

She couldn't tell him Lucas wasn't there. She didn't want the man to know she was alone. And she *was* alone. A quick glance next door to the Robertsons' didn't make her feel better. The big house was dark and there were no cars out front. And because the rain had only just stopped, no one was out walking their dog or enjoying the ocean view.

She really was alone in the dark with a man who didn't look very stable. If she called 911, she couldn't report a crime…he hadn't done anything. But if she didn't call and he did do something threatening, how stupid would she feel?

"Um, Lucas is in the backyard," she blurted.

"Fine," the man said and took another slow step, as if lifting each of his feet was taking every ounce of his strength. His words slurred as he vowed, "I'll jus' go she him."

Rose kept her gaze fixed on him but for a brief glance out to her car, parked at the curb. She decided she'd run out to it as soon as the man rounded the corner of the house. Once she was away, she'd call Lucas to tell him what was happening. She didn't want him to show up unaware of the man who clearly was looking for some kind of trouble.

Her stomach churned as she stood up, slowly. He didn't seem to notice her while he looked around as if trying to remember where he was and why. The heavy, cloying scent of too much beer hit her like a wave on the next breeze.

Suddenly, his bleary gaze shot to her and he demanded again, "Who're you?"

"A friend of Lucas's," she said, keeping her voice low as she moved carefully toward the steps.

The man snorted. "He don't have *friends*. No-good bastard…"

Instinctively, Rose wanted to defend Lucas, which would clearly be a mistake, since the man obviously was furious with him. She had to clamp her lips shut to keep from speaking, though.

So maybe she shouldn't wait to get to her car, Rose thought, and eased down the few steps to the paved walkway. He watched every move she made, and Rose almost wished it would start raining again. She would take every distraction she could get. "Well, I've got to leave now, so..."

She stepped off the walkway into the still-sodden grass, trying to keep distance between them. But for a swaying, unsteady drunk, the man moved quickly. He was suddenly at her side, holding on to her arm with an iron grip.

"Jus' wait a damn minute here, girly. You know Lucas."

"Yes," she said, holding her breath as much as possible. The stench of alcohol was much harsher now. And his breath was horrifying. As was his tight hold on her arm.

He was big and angry and drunk.

Not a good combination.

"You could talk to him. Tell him to not fire me." He leaned in closer, lost his balance and almost took them both down before somehow finding his footing again.

Rose's arm hurt where he held her, and her nerves jangled like sleigh bells. She tried to pull away, but the man was so much stronger than she was, she didn't have a hope. She still clutched her phone and as unobtrusively as she could, lifted it so she could see the dial pad.

"Hey! No phonin' him," the drunk told her and knocked the phone from her hand.

She glanced down at her phone, lying on the wet grass, and felt her heart slide down into the pit of her stomach.

"Let me call Lucas. He'll come talk to you," she urged, her voice as placating as she could make it, despite the fear. "Straighten all this out."

"Yeah?" He looked hopeful for a moment, but then his fingers tightened around her upper arm until she winced with a fresh wave of pain.

Then he shook his head. "No. He won't. Damn Kings. Once they make up their minds…"

"I can help." She tried again because really, what choice did she have? "Just let me try."

He thought about it for a long minute. Frowning, he staggered in place, caught himself, then finally nodded and released his grip on her arm. The pain of release was almost as sharp as it had been when he held her.

As soon as she was free, Rose bolted, leaving her phone on the grass. All she could think about was getting away. Getting help. Something. As she ran, she fumbled in her purse for her car keys.

Behind her, she heard the man shout *"Hey!"* and then the heavy pounding of his footsteps as he came after her. He was too drunk, too unsteady to move fast, though, she told herself. She had the advantage, if only she could—

Headlights flashed in her eyes and she threw one arm up in defense. A car screeched up to the curb behind hers and a moment later, Lucas was jumping out of his SUV.

"Rose? What's wrong?" His gaze shifted to the man coming after her. Instantly, Lucas pulled Rose to stand behind him, placing his body between her and any danger. "Warren, what are you doing here?"

"Came to talk," the man shouted. "Your lady there was helping me."

Even in the glare of the bright lights, Rose saw Lucas's features tighten into a mask of pure rage.

"Damn fool," he muttered, then looked over his shoulder at her. "Are you all right, Rose? Did he hurt you?"

"No. I'm fine."

He took a breath and released it as he nodded. "Good. That's good. Go to the house. Wait for me on the porch."

"No. I just want to go home, Lucas. I'm leaving."

He checked on Warren again, then took one moment to cup her cheek briefly. "Please. The porch."

Rose looked from him to Warren and then back again. She saw anger in Lucas's face, but she also saw worry, so she nodded. Heck, she was too shaken to drive anyway. Rose walked a wide circle around Warren and then hurried to the porch, pausing only long enough to snatch up her phone. From her safe vantage point, she watched Lucas with the other man.

Fisting his hands on his hips, Lucas said, "Warren, you shouldn't have come here."

The man scraped one hand across his face and to Rose's mind, he suddenly looked more miserable than scary. "Din't have choice. I can't lose my job," he said and dropped to the grass, cupping his head in his hands.

Lucas still looked furious, but there was also something of pity in his face as he looked down at the man. "If you were looking for a second chance, coming to my home, drunk, and threatening my woman aren't the ways to get it."

His woman?

Those two little words punched at her heart. Rose shivered, then before she could make too much of it, told herself it meant nothing. He was talking to a drunk. Making a point. And still those two words reverberated inside her like a shout into an echoing canyon.

"Din't hurt her," Warren muttered. "Wouldn't hurt a woman."

"That makes this your lucky night," Lucas told him and pulled out his phone. He glanced up at Rose as if satisfying himself that she was safe, then he made a brief call before tucking the phone back into his pocket.

"You stay right there, Warren," he ordered. "I swear, if you move from that spot…"

Warren didn't even flinch. Just sat on the wet grass cradling his head and murmuring to himself.

Clearly disgusted, Lucas walked to Rose, pulled her into his arms, then set her back from him and held her face between his palms. "Are you sure you're okay?"

"Yeah. He didn't really hurt me. Just seriously creeped me out." She gave a quick look to the now-moaning man on the lawn. "Who is he?"

Lucas glanced back at the man. "He worked for me. Until recently. I fired him. And by the smell of him, he's spent the past few days in a bar."

"Did you call the police?"

He looked back at her and sighed. "No. I called Sean. He'll drive Warren home. I don't want him arrested. He's got enough problems. But if he had hurt you…"

She shook her head. "He didn't."

Nodding, Lucas pulled out his keys, opened the front door and said, "Will you just wait for me inside? I've got to stay with Warren until Sean gets here."

She should go, Rose knew it. After all, she had only gone to his house to throw his check back in his face. But looking up at him how, she knew she wasn't leaving. At least, not yet. "I'll wait."

He gave her a smile, then turned back to the yard. He walked to Warren's side, then went down in a crouch beside the man. His words were too low for her to overhear, so Rose did as he asked and went into the house.

A half hour later, Sean had come and gone and Warren was on his way home. Lucas smiled grimly at the memory of Sean's disgust as they loaded Warren into his car. Lucas had no doubt that Warren was getting an earful on the drive home. Sean was as easygoing as they came, but tell him that a woman had been scared or hurt or in any way bothered, and Sean went coldly ballistic.

He wouldn't do anything to the man, but Lucas was willing to bet that after having Sean give him the shout-down of the century, Warren would accept being fired and disappear from their lives.

Walking into the house, Lucas could smell fresh coffee brewing, and he followed the scent straight back to the kitchen. He'd been avoiding that room, unable to even so much as enter it without Rose's memory rising up and nearly choking him.

So when he pushed the door open and saw her standing in the brilliantly lit room, she took his breath away. She'd draped her coat over a chair. She was wearing dark blue jeans, a red, wide-necked sweater and her long blond hair fell over her shoulders in a cascade of silk.

His fingers itched to touch her again. To feel the smooth slide of her skin. And because the urge was so strong, he jammed his hands into his pockets to keep from doing just that.

She turned when he entered and the edge of her sweater dipped low over one shoulder. That's when he saw the marks on her arm. Furious all over again, he was at her side in two long strides.

"Lucas?"

"You said he didn't hurt you," he muttered, pulling the sweater down far enough on her arm that he could see the prints of Warren's hard fingers on her pale skin. "He left marks, Rose. You'll be bruised by tomorrow."

"He didn't mean to," she said, wincing a little as Lucas's fingers moved over her arm.

"I should have had him arrested," Lucas muttered, lifting his gaze to hers.

"No, Lucas. He was just drunk and sad and scared..."

"He put his hands on you."

She reached up and touched his face, and Lucas felt the warmth of her slide down into that cold, empty pit he'd been carrying around in his stomach for days.

"I'm okay. Really."

He pulled in a breath, looked into her eyes and said, "When I saw you there. With him chasing you—"

"I was really glad you showed up when you did," she admitted.

"Me, too." His gaze moved over her face. Her scent filled him and Lucas gave into the need that had been plaguing him for days.

It was over. He knew that. Accepted it. But she was here and his body was hard and thirsting for her so badly he could hardly draw a breath.

"Rose..."

She shook her head even as she leaned into him. "Lucas, this isn't why I came here."

"I don't care," he admitted. "I just need to taste you again. To hold you again."

"We really shouldn't," she said and met him halfway as his mouth came down over hers.

Instant heat and hunger leaped up to snare both of them into a trap of their own design. He pulled her in tight, loving the feel of her body molding to his. She sighed into his mouth, and he took her breath and held it inside him, wanting to devour all of her.

His mind, his heart, his soul, begged to be heard, but

the only voice he listened to was that of his body. She was here. In his arms. Where he needed her.

Groaning, he shifted his hands to the waistband of her jeans, undid the snap and zipper and in seconds, was sliding one hand across her bare abdomen. She kissed him harder, deeper, her tongue twining with his in a desperate dance of desire.

He lowered his hand, beneath the elastic band of her panties and down to the heart of her that waited for him. She broke the kiss on a gasp and rocked her hips into him as he touched and stroked and explored her damp heat. Again and again, his fingers moved on her, taking her higher as he watched her eyes burn and then glaze over with what she was feeling. What she was giving him in this one stolen moment.

And when her body couldn't last another moment, when she was so taut with tension there was no higher for her to reach, Lucas felt the first shattering climax jolt through her.

"Lucas!" She clutched at his shoulders, fingers digging in as she moved on his hand, riding the waves of sensation that poured through her in a tidal wave of release.

Finally, only the slightest ripples remained, and she shivered as he held her close. Her face was flushed; her eyes unfocused; her breathing short and sharp. Finally, she licked her lips and let her head fall to his chest as if she were unable to hold it up on her own.

He kissed the top of her head and tried to calm his own racing heartbeat. It was a futile attempt. What he wanted was to bury himself inside her. To feel her heat holding him as closely and deeply as before. Pulling his hand free, he sighed and said, "Come with me, Rose. Upstairs."

A choked-off chuckle scraped from her throat, and she shook her head against his chest. "No."

"What?" He pulled back so he could look at her and waited until she lifted her gaze to his. "Why not?"

Biting her bottom lip, she moved away from him, zipped up her jeans and straightened her sweater. Then she pushed her hair back from her face. Looking up at him, she took a deep breath and blew it out again before trusting herself to speak.

"Because it wouldn't change anything." Another short laugh escaped her. "I shouldn't have let what just happened happen, either."

He grabbed her, then eased his hold when she winced as his hand came down on the bruises inflicted by Warren. Remembering that, knowing that she had been in danger and he hadn't been there until almost the last moment, terrified him and infused his words with a kind of desperation.

"But it did happen, Rose. You want me. I want you. Simple."

"No, it's not," she said sadly and it startled Lucas to see a sheen of tears fill her eyes. But she blinked them back so quickly, they were gone before he could even really ask himself why they had appeared in the first place. "It's not simple at all."

Frustration bubbled inside him. He was aching for want of her and was apparently going to keep on aching, he thought. So he blurted, "Then why the hell did you come here?"

She pulled away from him and a second later, steely determination was etched into her features. "Not for this," she told him.

Lucas drew a long, deep breath, fighting the hunger inside and the sense of annoyance he felt at her easy dismissal of what was clearly simmering between them. "Fine. *Why?*"

Lifting her chin, she walked past him to the table where she'd laid her purse. She opened it, pulled out an envelope and thrust it at him. "Because of this. I wanted to come over here and personally hand that back to you."

"What?" He glanced at it and recognized the envelope and check he'd sent her only the day before. He had deliberately sent her much more than he owed her, not because he was feeling guilty, either, but because he had simply wanted her to have it. Apparently, she hadn't appreciated it.

"Take it," she said, waving the damn envelope like a battle flag.

"I don't want it."

"Neither do I," she countered, and pushed it into one of his hands before folding her arms beneath her breasts.

His fingers tightened around the damn envelope, crushing it. "You earned the money."

"Hah! That's more than triple what you owe me for cooking lessons, and you know it. So the only other way I could possibly have *earned* that much was if—"

She left the rest of it unsaid but he didn't need to hear it. Insult slapped at him. "Are you serious? You think I'm *paying* you for sex?"

One shoulder lifted in a half-hearted shrug. But her eyes burned with an inner fire that singed Lucas with its strength.

"What else am I supposed to think?" she asked.

Offended down to his bones, Lucas felt his own anger rise to nearly choke him. Deliberately, he tore the check in two and threw both halves into the air, letting them fall to the gleaming wood floor at their feet. "There. Happy now?"

"Yes," she snapped, not even glancing at the torn check. "I'm happy. You can't *buy* me, Lucas. You can't pay me off. You can't assuage your conscience by writing a damn check as if I'm an overdue bill."

He just stared at her. What the hell was he supposed to say to something so outrageously *wrong?*

"That's not what I was doing, damn it!" His shout filled the room and seemed to bounce off the beamed ceiling.

She stepped up close, her gaze boring into his. "Then what? Why would you do it?"

Lucas shoved a hand through his hair. "I was trying to help."

She snorted.

"You're a damn good cook, Rose," he said, voice harsh as if every word was being scraped out of his throat. "You need money to build your business. I was... investing."

"Investing," she repeated, shaking her head at him in disbelief. "You wanted to invest in a woman you said you never wanted to see again? Where's the logic you're so fond of, Lucas? That doesn't make sense at all. But I'm supposed to just accept it?"

"Believe what you want," he muttered. *Try to do a nice thing and have it thrown back in your face,* he told himself. He never should have started any of this. It was all turning out to be far more trouble than it was worth. Now he was left trying to explain his motives to Rose when he didn't completely understand them himself.

Accepting the inevitable, he growled, "I'll mail you a check for what I owe you for the cooking lessons and leave it at that. All right?"

"Fine."

His gaze met hers.

Ice to fire.

"Then we're done here," he told her, grabbing hold of what was left of his pride and clinging to it.

"We're done, Lucas," she agreed, snatching up her jacket and slipping into it. She lifted her purse, slung it over her shoulder and walked out of the room, her heels clacking loudly on the wood floor.

From a distance, he heard the front door open, then close.

He was alone again.

Twelve

Two weeks later, Rose ran into the local coffee bar, her gaze scanning past the late-afternoon crowd, waiting in line, seated at tables. A wail of jazz piped down through overhead speakers and the scent of fresh coffee and doughnuts washed over her in welcome.

But today, nothing could soothe her. Not even doughnuts.

Quickly, she looked at the employees behind the counters, searching for the one person in the world she could really talk to. Just then, Delilah came out from the back room, laughing at one of her coworkers. She looked up, spotted Rose and called out, "Hi, sweetie! Having a latte emergency?"

A couple of people glanced at her, then turned away again and another barista, Eric, grinned a hello.

Rose hardly noticed. She hurried to the end of the

counter and waved Dee over. As she got closer, her friend's bright green eyes narrowed in concern.

Voice low, she asked, "Are you all right, Rose?"

"I'm *so* far away from all right," she muttered, glancing around to make sure no one else was close enough to listen in. "Can you take a break?"

"Sure," Dee told her, concern shifting to worry now as she half turned and said loudly, "Eric, I'm taking a break. Back in fifteen."

He nodded and Dee slipped around the counter, took Rose's arm and steered her out of the shop.

Outside, the sun was beginning to set and its rays seemed aimed at Rose's eyes. She squinted in response and took a long breath as she tried to ease the jumping nerves in the pit of her stomach. It didn't help.

"What is it, sweetie?"

"The end," Rose said dramatically.

"What?" Dee tugged her over to one of the tables gathered in front of Coffee Heaven.

After the storms they'd been having, the locals were out in force, enjoying the winter sun and the dry sidewalks. Kids rolled past on skateboards and women pushed babies in strollers. A golden retriever sat placidly beside its owner, who read the paper and pretended he had the whole world to himself.

Rose was only vaguely aware of all of it. There was too much running through her mind. Too many variables to consider, and one undeniable truth she had to face.

She swallowed hard and blurted out, "I'm pregnant."

"Oh, Rose…" Dee leaned forward and lowered her voice. "Are you sure?"

"Three test kits later," Rose said with a sigh, "I'm way sure."

A couple of minutes of silence passed before Dee sat back in her chair, keeping her gaze fixed on Rose. "So now what?"

"That's the problem. I know 'now what,' I just don't want to do it."

"Talk to Lucas, you mean."

"Yes."

"Honey, you've been making yourself sick missing him for the past two weeks," Dee said softly. "Is this really such bad news?"

"God, yes—I mean, no…I mean…" God, Rose thought, she wasn't even making sense to herself. But hardly surprising. Her brain had been in a spin since the last of the three tests had come back positive.

Seriously, what were the odds of getting pregnant on the *one time* a condom breaks? There were people all over the country—heck, the *world*—trying desperately to have children. She should feel blessed, she knew. And that feeling would eventually come. But right now, all she felt was worried.

Rose chewed at her fingernail, noticed what she was doing and stopped. "The baby isn't bad news, Dee. I mean, it's a surprise, but not a bad one, you know?"

Dee nodded, but kept quiet so Rose could talk and get her thoughts straight in her own mind. A truly *great* best friend, Rose thought.

"The bad news is, once I tell Lucas, he's going to want to marry me—"

"And that's bad because—"

"Because he doesn't love me," Rose muttered and glared at the newspaper-reading man when he flicked her a curious glance. Immediately, he hid behind the paper again. Rose lowered her voice. "He'll offer to marry me out of duty. Because me and the baby are his 'responsibility.' I don't want to be that to the man I love, you know? I want him to want me because he can't live without me. Not because a layer of latex failed at precisely the wrong moment." She paused, then started again before Dee could say a word. "If we get married for all the wrong reasons, it would turn out just like my marriage to Henry did."

"Henry was a horse's ass," Dee pointed out.

"True. But the bottom line is, I didn't love him. He didn't love me. And we created a gigantic ball of misery together. I don't want that with Lucas."

"But you *do* love him," Dee argued.

"Yes, I do. And how long before that feeling just withers and dies because I know he's thinking he was trapped into marrying me?" She shook her head as that thought settled in and turned her stomach. "This isn't the fifties. We have choices now, you know? And my choice is to *not* marry a man who doesn't love me just because he's the father of my child."

"Okay, I'm right there with you," Dee told her firmly. "Anything you decide is okay by me. So the next question is, what do you *want* to do?"

"Sadly," Rose said, slumping against the chair back, "*want* really doesn't come into it. If it did, then what I would want is Lucas and I together, celebrating a baby."

But that wasn't going to happen and Rose was just going to have to come to grips with the fact. Lucas had made his choice, and it hadn't been her. In the two weeks since she'd last seen him, she had heard nothing from him. Beyond a check she received for the exact amount owed her.

It was as if he'd shut her out so easily that he hadn't even missed her. Which was both sad and infuriating. Here she was, moping around, thinking about him, dreaming about him, carrying his *child,* and he was probably not even giving her a passing thought.

Instinctively, Rose squared her shoulders as if metaphorically accepting the weight that had just dropped onto her shoulders. No, Lucas wouldn't be back and if he did offer marriage, it wouldn't be the kind she wanted. He'd already made that very clear. So it would be best all the way around to put aside dreams and start getting ready for reality.

As that thought settled in, she knew one other person she had to tell before facing Lucas with the news.

"I have to go see Dave."

"Really?" Dee just stared at her, surprised. "You sure your brother is the one to help with this?"

Rose shrugged. "He's been better lately. Since we had that talk and finally came clean with each other, we've sort of found a new and richer relationship. He comes over a lot now, and he does know about me and Lucas, so this won't be a shock." She stopped and smiled sadly. "I have to tell him. He's my family."

"Okay," Dee said and stood up when Rose did. "But if he lets you down by being an idiot about this, just call me."

Far from being the Mayor of Idiotville, Dave was the perfect older brother. Once Rose told him what was going on, he said and did all the right things. He was supportive and understanding and Rose was so grateful she could have cried. Now that there were no more secrets between them, she knew she could depend on him. And Rose was going to need him in the next few months and then beyond even that.

"Don't worry," he told her, giving her a hug that

reassured and comforted all at the same time. "Everything's gonna be fine."

"I hope you're right."

"I'm always right," Dave teased, pulling back to look down into her eyes.

She laughed as he meant her to. "Oh, yeah. Now I remember."

"Atta girl," he said, a quick smile flashing across his features. "We're Clancys, you and me. We can handle anything. And your baby will be just fine, I swear it."

"Thanks, Dave," she said, leaning into him just to feel the solid strength of him. She was so tired, she could hardly stand up. It was as if all of her energy was going directly to worrying about the new life she carried inside. It was exhausting. "I'm so thankful I can count on you."

"Always," he promised, then asked, "Have you told Lucas?"

"No." She pulled away, wrapped her arms around herself and dropped into the corner of her couch. Drawing her legs up beneath her, she shook her head for emphasis. "Not yet. I know I have to, but I'm not ready to talk to him right now."

"Okay…"

Something in his tone alerted her, and she snapped him a look. "I don't want you talking to him, either. I'm going to be the one to tell him, Dave. And I'll do it my way, all right?"

"Sure. Absolutely."

Her gaze narrowed on him, looking for some sign that he didn't mean what he was saying, but he just looked… supportive. For which she was grateful. Even knowing that she would be sharing custody with Lucas, raising a baby on her own was a daunting prospect. She was going to need moral support for the journey, and she was so grateful to know that her brother was on her side.

"Thanks for understanding."

"You bet, Rose," he said softly. "I'm here for you. Whatever you need."

"Right now," she said, with a rueful smile, "I think I need a nap. It's been a full day."

"Yeah," he said, walking over to her. He bent down to kiss the top of her head. "You do that. I'll lock your door when I leave."

"Okay." She scooted down on the couch and rested her head on one of the throw pillows. "And Dave... thanks again."

"Don't worry about a thing."

She was practically asleep by the time he walked out the front door.

So there was no way she could have seen his expression shift from that of concerned older brother to one of icy determination. She wasn't ready to talk to Lucas? She didn't have to be. Dave was *more* than ready.

He had a lot to say to his old friend, and there was no time like the present.

"These are *great*," Sean said, reaching for another steak-and-cheese quesadilla. He burned his fingers and hissed in a breath as he dropped the food onto his plate. Grinning at Rafe and Lucas, he said, "You gotta give it up for Rose. If she can teach *you* to cook, she deserves some kind of medal."

"He's right," Rafe said, leaning back in his chair and reaching out to grab his beer. "Even though it wasn't your 'plan,' you managed to learn how to cook. Impressive."

"Yeah. Real impressive." He could cook, but he had no one to cook for. Which was why when it was his turn to host the weekly King meeting, he had volunteered to make his brothers dinner. Now, he couldn't remember why he had offered. Being in this room, even using that new cast-iron skillet he had bought on Rose's orders, left him feeling…incomplete, somehow. As if there was something important missing from his house. His *life*.

Lucas looked at his brothers, then let his gaze track around the kitchen he rarely set foot in these days.

Just being in the room was tearing at him. How the hell could he ever relax in here when Rose was stamped all over the place? Her scent, her laughter and, God help him, since that last night he'd been with her, even her passion was etched indelibly onto this room.

In fact, everywhere he went in his house, he heard her, saw her, tasted her. He wasn't even sleeping in his own bed anymore because he would wake up in the middle of the night stretching out his arms to her and finding only emptiness. How could his life have come so undone in a matter of weeks? How had the home he loved become foreign to him?

His sanctuary had become a prison of his own making.

"You're not eating much," Rafe mused.

"Not hungry, I guess," Lucas said with a shrug. In fact, he hadn't been hungry for two weeks. The knot in his guts made the thought of food impossible. Understandable, he told himself frequently. Of course, he'd have an adjustment period after cutting Rose out of his life. But he was sure it would right itself. Eventually.

"Right." Rafe took a sip of beer and said, "So, Warren stopped by my office this morning."

Lucas shot him a look. "And you're just mentioning

this now? Why the hell didn't you tell me he was there today?"

"Take it easy." Rafe ignored the heat in Lucas's voice and continued, "The man's feeling like a fool and only came to see me to apologize in person."

"Notice he didn't apologize to you," Sean said with a grin. "Probably afraid you'd drop him again."

"I should have had him arrested," Lucas countered, remembering again the bruises on Rose's arm. her slight shivers as he raced up to find her alone, facing a drunk in the dark. "He scared the crap out of Rose that night."

"I know," Rafe said quietly. "He knows it, too, and he's ashamed. Actually, I almost fell out of my chair when I heard that man say out loud for the first time ever, *it's my fault.*"

"About time," Lucas muttered.

Rafe nodded. "He also asked that I apologize for him to both you and Rose, Lucas. And to tell you that you won't have any more trouble from him. He's moving back to Phoenix to start over."

Lucas was glad to hear that Warren was leaving town. He didn't want that guy anywhere near Rose. Not that she would ever know Warren had left. How would she? Lucas wouldn't be seeing her again so he could tell her. Ever.

Absently, he rubbed the middle of his chest at a mystery ache that seemed to have lodged itself there.

"Another miracle chalked up to Rose," Sean said. "Because of her, Warren stepped up to the plate and took responsibility for the first time in his life. She really is an amazing woman."

"Yeah," Lucas agreed somberly. "She is."

"So what're you going to do about it?" Rafe asked.

"What?" Lucas looked back and forth between his

brothers and noted they both wore the same expression. Exhausted patience.

"Come on," Sean said, taking another bite of his third quesadilla. "We're not stupid. We can actually see the difference in you since you stopped seeing Rose."

"I don't know what you're talking about."

"Sure you don't," Rafe said with a smirk. "Hell, even your secretary's complaining about your tiger-with-a-toothache personality lately."

"Yeah," Sean added. "Evelyn says she's going to start force feeding you Katie's cookies to try to sweeten you up."

Lucas scowled at both of them, and if his secretary were there, he'd have one for her, too. He didn't appreciate being talked about or wondered over. His personal life was no one's business but his own. They could all damn well butt out.

"But cookies won't do it, will they?" Rafe asked quietly, gaze locked on Lucas. "It's Rose. It's been Rose all along."

Yes, it was Rose.

It was always Rose.

She never left his mind. The gaping hole in his heart reminded him with every beat that she was gone. That he'd let her go. Hell, that he'd actually *walked away* from her. And why? Because of his stupid plan.

You can't plan your life that way, and he knew it. What was that quote of John Lennon's? *Life is what happens when you're busy making other plans.* That about summed it up. Lucas had planned to live his life alone. To never get entangled in the silky webs of love and marriage. To avoid any relationship that even looked remotely long-term.

And that had worked out well for him.

Until Rose.

Lucas had spent the past two weeks fighting every instinct he had that demanded he go to her. Hold her. Kiss her. No other woman had ever made him want her so much—even out of bed. Rose challenged him, laughed with him, argued with him and stood up to him, willing to go toe-to-toe with him, even when he was *right*, damn it.

And he missed her more than he would have thought possible.

Suddenly irritated with not just himself, but also his interfering brothers, Lucas pushed up from his chair. "I don't need an intervention or whatever the hell this is."

"Oh, hell yes, you do," Sean said with a grin. "You're a pain in the ass to be around, Lucas. More so even than usual."

He gave him a snide smile. "Thanks."

"You're in love with her."

Lucas gaped at Rafe. "I am not."

Sean laughed, and Lucas shifted his glare to him.

"Yes, you are," Rafe said amiably. "Think I don't recognize the signs? Wasn't so long ago that I was doing with Katie exactly what you're doing now with Rose. And I'm here to tell you that hiding from it or ignoring it won't make those feelings disappear."

"It's worth a shot," Lucas mumbled.

"That's where you're wrong," Rafe told him. "You think you're miserable now? Wait another month or two. Or a year. You'll still be torn up in knots over Rose and torturing yourself uselessly. Face it," he added with a smile, "when a King falls for a woman, he stays fallen. There's no escape."

"Damn, that sounds terrifying," Sean said, to no one in particular.

Rafe ignored him and focused his gaze directly on Lucas. "A *smart* man wouldn't want to escape."

Was he smart? Lucas wondered. Or was Rafe reading too much into this? Seeing love where only need existed? What the hell did Lucas know about love? He had never felt it before. How could he be sure that was what he was feeling now? Need and desire were so twisted up inside him, he wasn't sure of anything anymore.

Which was damned lowering to admit, even to himself.

Meeting his brother's stoic stare took every ounce of willpower Lucas had in him. Rafe saw too much. Knew too much. And Lucas couldn't hide the truth any longer. Not from Rafe. Not from himself.

This aching, gaping hole inside him was what was left after he carved Rose out of his life. And if he didn't get her back, the emptiness would eventually swallow him. He'd be forced to live a half life, always wondering what might have been.

"If you want my advice," Rafe said a second later, "and even if you don't…go see Rose. Do some groveling. Get her back while you still have the chance."

Sean snorted. "Lucas? *Apologize?*"

"If he's got half a brain," Rafe said, still staring into Lucas's eyes, "then yeah."

Thankfully, he was spared having to reply when the doorbell rang. He left his brothers arguing over whether or not Lucas had half a brain and stomped through the house to the front door. He didn't bother to look outside first to see who it was. He was too damned grateful for the timely interruption.

If he had looked, he might have had time to duck.

As it was, Dave Clancy's punch caught him squarely on the jaw and staggered Lucas back several steps.

Seeing stars, Lucas cupped his jaw and shouted, "What the hell?"

"You son of a bitch." Dave stalked toward him, ready to deliver another blow when Rafe and Sean came running down the hall.

"What's going on?" Rafe demanded.

Sean was already moving to Lucas's side, presenting a united King front.

Dave's furious gaze never shifted from Lucas. "He knows what's going on. Ask him."

"I don't know what you're talking about!" Lucas glared at him. "I opened the door, you hit me. End of story."

"You didn't see that coming?" Sean muttered.

Lucas shot him a murderous look before turning back to Dave. "What are you doing here? And why the hell did you slug me?"

"Rose is pregnant."

Three little words, dropped into the room, and it was as if a bomb had gone off.

Sean gave a low whistle.

Rafe grumbled something under his breath.

Dave looked like he wanted to go another round.

And Lucas had never been so happy about anything in his life. Dave's news had hit Lucas harder than the man's fist had. His mind raced. Rose. Pregnant. He was going to be a father. And something else. He was going to be a *husband*.

That word settled into him and to his surprise didn't rattle him much at all. Finally, he had a *reason* to marry Rose. To make sure she married him. He would accept nothing less.

Despite the pain in his jaw, he grinned.

Dave saw it and frowned. "You think this is funny?"

"Hell, no," Lucas told him, rubbing the ache in his jaw again. "Nothing funny at all about this. But it's the best news I've ever had."

"I think he's got a concussion," Sean murmured.

"No," Rafe said, smiling, "I think he just figured out what he really wants."

"Damn straight," Lucas told him, then looked at Dave again. Rose's brother. They would all be family soon, he told himself, and made a point to ease the protective streak Dave was displaying. "Look. You and I, we straightened a few things out between us, right?"

"Yeah…"

"And I told you then that I started the affair with Rose as a way of getting some payback on you."

Dave nodded and didn't look real happy with that reminder.

"Things changed," Lucas said simply. "Rose is… everything to me." God, it felt good to admit it. To say out loud what his heart and soul had been trying to tell him for weeks. "I'm going to get her to marry me, Dave. As fast as I can."

The other man studied him for a long moment before finally nodding his head in acceptance. "She won't be easy to convince. She doesn't take orders from anyone anymore."

Lucas laughed. "Believe me, I know."

"But if it means anything to you," Dave added, holding out his right hand, "you've got my blessing."

Stunned to realize that it did indeed mean a lot, Lucas shook his old friend's hand, then turned to his brothers. "I've gotta go. Lock up when you leave."

As he ran out to his car, he heard Sean ask, "So, now that we're almost related, you want a beer?"

Lucas drove straight to Rose's house. He probably should have stopped at a jewelry store so he could hold a big, shiny diamond out to her when he announced that they'd be getting married…but he couldn't wait that long.

He felt better than he had in two weeks. The ache in his chest was gone. His eyes were clear and his heart, mind and body were finally in agreement on something.

Rose was the woman for him.

No one else would ever do.

Spotting the ridiculous skillet car in her driveway, Lucas grinned, parked out front and ran to the front door. The streetlights shone down on the narrow street filled with tiny houses and even tinier yards. People were so close together here, he thought they could probably shout "Bless you" when their neighbor sneezed.

He pounded on the door a few times, then hit the doorbell just for good measure.

Rocking on his heels, he looked around while he waited. Next door, an older woman was holding one end of a leash while an ancient-looking beagle wandered aimlessly around the yard looking for a place to go.

The woman frowned at him when he rang the bell again, and Lucas grinned. Her expression didn't change, and he shrugged, turning back to face the door, still closed and locked to him. What was taking her so long? The house was so small she wouldn't need more than a minute to get to the front door from anywhere in the place.

"Rose!"

Silence, but for the hiss from the older woman next door. Lucas ignored her.

"Rose, I know you're there, talk to me!"

"No!" The answering shout came from the other side of the door, and he smiled at the sound of her irritable, contrary voice.

His world suddenly straightened itself out. And he had to wonder how he had managed to be so clueless for so long. All he really needed was Rose. It was all so simple. So perfect.

Or, it would be, if he could get her to open the damn door.

Leaning his hands on either side of the door, he said, "Let me in, Rose. We have to talk."

"There's nothing to talk about," she told him.

"Not according to Dave," he called back.

"That traitor."

"Rose, let me in."

"Go away."

"Not gonna happen. Not again," he swore vehemently, his gaze raking over the door as if trying to see past it to the woman on the other side. "Not ever."

"Lucas, this changes nothing," she said after a long, tense moment of silence.

"Everything's changed and damn it," he said, "if you won't let me in, then I'll just shout it to you through this bloody door!"

"You watch your language, young man!"

This from the neighbor. Lucas turned a glance her way, then focused on Rose again. He didn't have time to worry about who else was listening. All that mattered was making sure that *Rose* heard every word.

Remembering Rafe's advice, Lucas figured she was owed some groveling. Strangely enough, it wasn't as hard as he might have imagined it would be. It was too important. Too necessary to be difficult.

"I know I hurt you, and I'm sorry." His voice dropped from a shout, but was still loud enough for her to hear him, he hoped. "I was stupid. Shortsighted. I thought I needed revenge when all I really needed was *you*."

"Lucas..."

She sounded tired. Defeated. A word he never would have associated with Rose Clancy before this. And it cut him deep that he had brought such a strong, wonderful woman such grief.

"Rose, give me the chance to show you what you mean to me. I won't blow it again," he shouted. "Damn it, Rose, I *love* you. Did you hear that, Rose? I love you."

He glared at the door that stood between him and the woman he needed to see. To hold.

"The least you could do is open the blasted door so I can tell you to your face what you mean to me!"

"That's it for you," the woman next door called out. "I'm calling the police!"

"Go ahead!" Lucas shouted. "Maybe *they* can make her open the door!"

Instantly, he heard locks turn and then the door was thrown open and Rose stepped out onto the porch. She was wearing the faded jeans he loved to see on her and a V-necked shirt that dipped low enough to display the tops of her breasts. Her hair was back in a ponytail again, and her beautiful blue eyes were red-rimmed from crying.

A stab of something sharp jabbed him in the chest and he swore silently that he would do whatever he could to see that she never cried again.

"It's okay, Mrs. Klein," Rose called to the neighbor,

who was dragging her old dog to the house. "We don't need the police, but thank you!"

The older woman glared at Lucas again and sniffed loudly, but allowed her dog to go back about his business.

Rose gave Lucas a long look before stepping into the house and saying, "Come in."

She was still reeling from his confession. She had never hoped to hear him say "I love you." Oh, all right, she had hoped. But hadn't thought it would ever really happen. Not Lucas King. Not the man who claimed not to believe in love or marriage or any of the things that were so inherently important to Rose.

Closing the door behind them, Rose looked up at him and saw something new in his eyes. Something that gave her chills. Something that told her maybe *hope* wasn't an impossible word after all.

"God, I've missed you," Lucas said, his voice deep and raw with emotion.

Rose wanted more than anything to go to him. To feel his arms come around her. To nestle her head on his chest and listen to the steady beat of his heart. But she couldn't. Not until she was sure he had meant what he said. She simply didn't think she could take another heartbreak.

"Dave shouldn't have told you about the baby," she finally said.

"You're right," Lucas agreed, reaching out to gently skim his fingertips along her jawline. "You should have."

"I was going to," she said. "I just wanted a few days to let the news settle in for me first."

He frowned suddenly. "Are you upset? About the baby, I mean?"

"No." She said it quickly. Firmly. Placing both hands on her flat abdomen, she shook her head and said again. "No, I'm not."

"I'm glad."

"But Lucas, this doesn't mean you have to marry me." God, those words cost her. All she really wanted was to be his wife. To raise their child together. To be loved by the man she loved with all of her heart.

"You're right." He closed the distance between them, laid both hands on her shoulders and said softly, "I don't *have* to marry you Rose. I *need* to marry you."

"Lucas—"

"Not because of the baby," he told her with a half smile that tugged at her heart. "But because without you, there's nothing. These past two weeks without you were the longest of my life. I fought every day to keep from coming here," he admitted. "I told myself I didn't need anyone. That what you and I had was just a temporary blip on the radar. I was wrong. I was an idiot to ever walk away from you."

"I want to believe you, Lucas. So much, I want to believe." Her heart felt as though it was being squeezed by a tight, cold fist. Her stomach was spinning and her mind raced with possibilities she couldn't quite bring herself to count on. Not yet.

"Then do," he insisted, pulling her into the circle of his arms, where she most wanted to be. "Rose, I told you a little of how I grew up."

She nodded, not wanting to speak, or interrupt him now, when every word spoken mattered.

"Well, I never believed love really existed. Never saw it, up close and personal. Then you walked into my life and suddenly, nothing was the same. You changed me. You changed everything. Forever."

She rested her forehead against the center of his chest and bit down hard on her bottom lip. This was all so good, she was afraid to take the chance. He was saying everything she had hoped he would and still, a part of her held back, worried and too cowardly to take the next step—trusting him to mean what he had said.

Tears welled in her eyes and choked her throat as she whispered, "I just don't want you to be saying all of this because of the baby."

"I'm not, Rose," he insisted, shifting so that he could cup her face between his palms and tip her face up to his. Gently, his thumbs rubbed away the tears that spilled from her eyes. "I'm saying all of this because of you. Who you are. What you've given me. What I want us to give each other. I love you, Rose Clancy. I always will."

A wave of love so rich and thick she could hardly breathe moved through her, and Rose could only stare up at him through her tears.

"I want this baby, Rose," he said, bending to press one brief, heartfelt kiss to her mouth. "And all the others that will come after it…"

"All?" she asked on a laugh.

He grinned and added, "But make no mistake, ever. You are the prize for me, Rose. You are the heart and soul of me. You are all I will ever need. Without you, I have nothing. With you, I have the world."

"I love you so much, Lucas," Rose whispered.

"Thank God," he said on a heavy sigh. "You had me worried, I can tell you."

She smiled up at him. "I never want to be apart from you again. These past two weeks were just so lonely."

"Then marry me, Rose." He kissed her again, harder, deeper, letting the passion between them sizzle and burn like a promise. "Come and live with me in that big, empty house. Help me make it a real home. For both of us."

"I will marry you," she said, finally giving in to the magic that was happening. Somehow, her world had righted itself again. She believed. In love. In Lucas. And in the life they would build together. "And I promise, that beautiful old house won't be empty for long."

* * * * *

COMING NEXT MONTH

Available November 8, 2011

#2119 WANTED BY HER LOST LOVE
Maya Banks
Pregnancy & Passion

#2120 TEMPTATION
Brenda Jackson
Texas Cattleman's Club: The Showdown

#2121 NOTHING SHORT OF PERFECT
Day Leclaire
Billionaires and Babies

#2122 RECLAIMING HIS PREGNANT WIDOW
Tessa Radley

#2123 IMPROPERLY WED
Anna DePalo

#2124 THE PRICE OF HONOR
Emilie Rose

REQUEST YOUR FREE BOOKS!

2 FREE NOVELS PLUS 2 FREE GIFTS!

Harlequin *Desire*

ALWAYS POWERFUL, PASSIONATE AND PROVOCATIVE

YES! Please send me 2 FREE Harlequin Desire® novels and my 2 FREE gifts (gifts are worth about $10). After receiving them, if I don't wish to receive any more books, I can return the shipping statement marked "cancel." If I don't cancel I will receive 6 brand-new novels every month and be billed just $4.30 per book in the U.S. or $4.99 per book in Canada. That's a saving of at least 14% off the cover price! It's quite a bargain! Shipping and handling is just 50¢ per book in the U.S. and 75¢ per book in Canada.* I understand that accepting the 2 free books and gifts places me under no obligation to buy anything. I can always return a shipment and cancel at any time. Even if I never buy another book, the two free books and gifts are mine to keep forever.

225/326 HDN FEF3

Name	(PLEASE PRINT)	
Address		Apt. #
City	State/Prov.	Zip/Postal Code

Signature (if under 18, a parent or guardian must sign)

Mail to the Reader Service:

IN U.S.A.: P.O. Box 1867, Buffalo, NY 14240-1867
IN CANADA: P.O. Box 609, Fort Erie, Ontario L2A 5X3

Not valid for current subscribers to Harlequin Desire books.

**Want to try two free books from another line?
Call 1-800-873-8635 or visit www.ReaderService.com.**

* Terms and prices subject to change without notice. Prices do not include applicable taxes. Sales tax applicable in N.Y. Canadian residents will be charged applicable taxes. Offer not valid in Quebec. This offer is limited to one order per household. All orders subject to credit approval. Credit or debit balances in a customer's account(s) may be offset by any other outstanding balance owed by or to the customer. Please allow 4 to 6 weeks for delivery. Offer available while quantities last.

Your Privacy—The Reader Service is committed to protecting your privacy. Our Privacy Policy is available online at www.ReaderService.com or upon request from the Reader Service.

We make a portion of our mailing list available to reputable third parties that offer products we believe may interest you. If you prefer that we not exchange your name with third parties, or if you wish to clarify or modify your communication preferences, please visit us at www.ReaderService.com/consumerschoice or write to us at Reader Service Preference Service, P.O. Box 9062, Buffalo, NY 14269. Include your complete name and address.

HDES11B

Harlequin® Special Edition® is thrilled to present a new installment in USA TODAY *bestselling author RaeAnne Thayne's reader-favorite miniseries,* THE COWBOYS OF COLD CREEK.

Join the excitement as we meet the Bowmans—four siblings who lost their parents but keep family ties alive in Pine Gulch. First up is Trace. Only two things get under this rugged lawman's skin: beautiful women and secrets. And in Rebecca Parsons, he finds both!

Read on for a sneak peek of CHRISTMAS IN COLD CREEK. *Available November 2011 from Harlequin® Special Edition®.*

On impulse, he unfolded himself from the bar stool. "Need a hand?"

"Thank you! I…" She lifted her gaze from the floor to his jeans and then raised her eyes. When she identified him her hazel eyes turned from grateful to unfriendly and cold, as if he'd somehow thrown the broken glasses at her head.

He also thought he saw a glimmer of panic in those interesting depths, which instantly stirred his curiosity like cream swirling through coffee.

"I've got it, Officer. Thank you." Her voice was several degrees colder than the whirl of sleet outside the windows.

Despite her protests, he knelt down beside her and began to pick up shards of broken glass. "No problem. Those trays can be slippery."

This close, he picked up the scent of her, something fresh and flowery that made him think of a mountain meadow on a July afternoon. She had a soft, lush mouth and for one brief, insane moment, he wanted to push aside that stray lock of hair slipping from her ponytail and taste her. Apparently he needed to spend a lot less time working and a great deal *more* time recreating with the opposite sex if he could have sudden random fantasies about a woman he wasn't even inclined to like, pretty or not.

"I'm Trace Bowman. You must be new in town."

She didn't answer immediately and he could almost see the wheels turning in her head. Why the hesitancy? And why that little hint of unease he could see clouding the edge of her gaze? His presence was obviously making her uncomfortable and Trace couldn't help wondering why.

"Yes. We've been here a few weeks."

"Well, I'm just up the road about four lots, in the white house with the cedar shake roof, if you or your daughter need anything." He smiled at her as he picked up the last shard of glass and set it on her tray.

Definitely a story there, he thought as she hurried away. He just might need to dig a little into her background to find out why someone with fine clothes and nice jewelry, and who so obviously didn't have experience as a waitress, would be here slinging hash at The Gulch. Was she running away from someone? A bad marriage?

So…Rebecca Parsons. Not Becky. An intriguing woman. It had been a long time since one of those had crossed his path here in Pine Gulch.

Trace won't rest until he finds out Rebecca's secret, but will he still have that same attraction to her once he does? Find out in CHRISTMAS IN COLD CREEK. Available November 2011 from Harlequin® Special Edition®.

Discover two classic tales of romance in one
incredible volume from

USA TODAY **Bestselling Author**

Catherine
Mann

Two powerful, passionate men
are determined to win back the women
who haunt their dreams...but it will
take more than just seduction
to convince them that this love will last.

IRRESISTIBLY HIS

Available October 25, 2011.